Some legends are true.

It is a myth out of history, spawned by Native American lore and the stories of Spanish Explorers. But what if the legends are true? Former Navy SEAL turned treasure hunter Uriah "Bones" Bonebrake sets off on his first solo adventure in this action-packed novella.

When television host Joanna Slater hires Bones to help investigate one of Florida's oldest and best-known legends, their crew gets more than they bargained for. Mystery and thrills abound in PRIMITIVE!

PRAISE FOR DAVID WOOD
AND THE DANE MADDOCK ADVENTURES

"Rip roaring action from start to finish. Wit and humor throughout. How soon until the next one? Because I can't wait." *Graham Brown, author of Shadows of the Midnight Sun*

"What an adventure! A great read that provides lots of action, and thoughtful insight as well, into strange realms that are sometimes best left unexplored." *Paul Kemprecos, author of Cool Blue Tomb and the NUMA Files*

"A page-turning yarn blending high action, Biblical speculation, ancient secrets, and nasty creatures. Indiana Jones better watch his back!" *Jeremy Robinson, author of SecondWorld*

"With the thoroughly enjoyable way Mr. Wood has mixed speculative history with our modern day pursuit of truth, he has created a story that thrills and makes one think beyond the boundaries of mere fiction and enter the world of 'why not'?" *David L. Golemon, Author of Ancients, Event, Legend, and Leviathan*

"A twisty tale of adventure and intrigue that never lets up and never lets go!" *Robert Masello, author of Bestiary and Blood and Ice*

"Let there be no confusion: David Wood is the next Clive Cussler. Once you start reading, you won't be able to stop until the last mystery plays out in the final line." *Edward G. Talbot, author of 2012: The Fifth World*

"I like my thrillers with lots of explosions, global locations and a mystery where I learn something new. Wood delivers! Recommended as a fast paced, kick ass read." *J.F. Penn, author of Desecration*

"Dourado is a brisk read, reminiscent of early Cussler adventures, and perfect for an afternoon at the beach or a cross-country flight. You'll definitely want more of Maddock." *Sean Ellis- Author of Into the Black*

"All the adventure, twists, and surprises you could hope for in an action series." *Kane Gilmour author of Resurrect*

PRIMITIVE

A BONES BONEBRAKE ADVENTURE

DAVID WOOD

Primitive, A Bones Bonebrake Adventure
Published by Adrenaline Press
www.adrenaline.press
Adrenaline Press is an imprint of Gryphonwood Press
Copyright 2015 by David Wood

ISBN-13: 978-1545191125
ISBN-10: 1545191123

BOOKS BY DAVID WOOD

The Dane Maddock Adventures
Dourado
Cibola
Quest
Icefall
Buccaneer
Atlantis
Ark
Xibalba
Loch (forthcoming)

Dane and Bones Origins
Freedom
Hell Ship
Splashdown
Dead Ice
Liberty
Electra
Amber
Justice
Treasure of the Dead

Jade Ihara Adventures (with Sean Ellis)
Oracle
Changeling

Bones Bonebrake Adventures
Primitive
The Book of Bones

FROM THE AUTHOR

Thanks for reading Primitive! This novella was originally intended to be a bonus short story to go along with a bundle of Maddock stories, but Bones wouldn't allow himself to be contained in so small a package. I've also included Aztlan, a Maddock and Bones short story that takes place after the events of Quest. I hope you enjoy both of them as much as I enjoyed writing them! Also, thanks to Nigel Gambles for letting me immortalize him within these pages.

David

PROLOGUE

1575- Off the Coast of La Florida

The storm raged. The wind shrieked in a banshee wail. Lightning shredded the slate gray blanket of clouds that hung low over the churning sea. The *San Amaro* pitched and rolled, her heavily laden holds causing her to ride low in the water, the icy waves breaking again and again over her decks.

Miguel de Morales squinted against the chill wind and icy rain. The temperature had dropped precipitously since the storm that had been brewing all day finally broke with the fury of a thousand hells. He clutched the ship's wheel, trying to keep her on a southeasterly course that would take them around the tip of La Florida and back out to the Atlantic.

"Captain, do you want me to take the wheel?" Dominic, his first mate, shouted to be heard above the howling wind. Rain streamed down his face like funeral tears and he staggered to maintain his footing on the tilting deck.

Morales shook his head. "The helm is mine until we get out of this storm." He didn't need to add *if we get out at all.*

"Very well." Dominic turned to look out at the roiling waves. "I've never seen anything like this. Not even out in the ocean."

Morales had to agree. This was, without a doubt, the worst storm at sea he'd ever encountered. He'd already ordered the sails be furled to prevent a broken mast or, worse, the ship capsizing. Now they were swept along by the wind and current, struggling to keep some control over the direction of their ship.

"What kind of storm can carry a ship this size along like a bobbing cork?" Dominic shouted.

Morales had no answer. The truth was, he was deathly afraid, but he could not let it show. He was the captain and, as such, must lead both in word and deed. If he feigned confidence, so might his crew.

The faint sound of cries from the foredeck drifted back to his place at the helm. "See what that's about."

Dominic nodded but before he could take a step, a small voice cried out in the darkness.

"Captain, we see land ahead!" A short, slender young man of a dozen years melted out of the darkness. Eugenio was Morales' page and his nephew. The young man had no business being out on the deck in this storm, but the boy was determined to become an apprentice sailor as soon as he was old enough, and insisted on acting as if he were already a full member of the crew. He turned and pointed forward. "There, off the port bow."

Morales strained to see what his nephew had spotted. The *San Amaro* rose on a swell, and in the next flash of lightning he saw the low-slung silhouette of a *cayo*, one of the small islands formed atop a coral reef that lined the south and west coasts of La Florida.

"We are closer to shore than I thought," Dominic said.

Morales didn't answer. He'd performed quick mental calculations and realized they were headed directly toward the southern tip of the *cayo*. What was more, even if he managed to steer *San Amaro* around the *cayo*, another of the low-lying islands lay just to the south. They had only a small gap through which to safely pass. Of course, he didn't know what lay beyond, but that was a problem for later.

"Tell everyone to get down below!" he called to Eugenio. "There is nothing more they can do here." While the possibility of being run aground on the *cayo* was very real, at least in that situation the crew would stand a chance of surviving such a fate. Should a man be swept overboard, death was a virtual certainty. Even those who were capable swimmers could not remain afloat in this churning, black maelstrom.

Eugenio turned and ran for the bow. He'd barely made it ten paces when the wave struck. A massive wall of water like the hand of Satan reaching up from the depths of Hell reared up on the port side. It swept across the deck, scooped the young man up, and carried him over the starboard rail and into the sea.

"Eugenio!" Morales cried. Brief, irrational flickers of thought flashed through his mind like fireflies. *Turn the boat around. Toss the boy a rope. Go in after him.* They were all absurd, of course. The ship was virtually beyond his control and Eugenio would be dead in a matter of seconds, a minute at most.

Perhaps he should shed a tear for his sister's oldest child, but present circumstances were too dire for such sentiments. He would do his best to keep his crew alive, and if he succeeded, mourn Eugenio at his leisure.

"Get below!" he shouted to Dominic.

"No, Captain. I'll be here to take the wheel if something should happen to you."

Morales gave a single nod. The man spoke sense and

there was no time for arguing.

The lightning flashed again, silhouetting the dark fingers of the twin *cayos* that seemed to reach out to grab *San Amaro.* Morales leaned on the wheel, trying to gain even a small measure of control against the force of the storm. He gritted his teeth and strained with every muscle, every last drop of energy. His body, soaked with rain, sweat, and sea water, trembled with the effort. He tasted salt in his mouth, felt the shiver of the cold wind, and wondered if these were the last sensations he would ever experience on this earth.

The shadowy form of the *cayo* loomed directly ahead, seemingly coming closer with each flash of lightning. Dominic hit the deck as they surged forward, carried on the crest of a wave.

Down they came, crashing into the angry sea.

And then they were past the island and its sharp coral reef. Dominic clambered to his feet and let out a whoop of delight. But it wasn't over.

The force of the storm, powerful beyond belief, continued to drive them forward as if by a supernatural force. The ship swept through the small bay and directly toward land.

"This cannot be happening," Morales whispered.

"This storm is the devil's work!" Dominic shouted.

Morales couldn't disagree. Helpless, he watched the shore approach, the thick tree line standing dark and sinister in the stormy night. What would happen when they ran aground?

And then he saw it.

"A river!" A dark channel wound back into the mainland and disappeared from sight. Could they make it?

The surge carried *San Amaro* past the shoreline and up the narrow river that fed into the bay. Morales could not help but marvel at the force required to sweep their galleon upstream against the current. But his wonder did not last. They came to a bend in the river and *San Amaro,* despite his best efforts, did not make the turn.

Morales cried out in rage and dove to the deck as their ship smashed into the forest. The masts snapped with ear-splitting cracks. The sound of splitting wood rang in his ears as the heavy galleon ripped limbs from trees and boards split from the force of repeated collisions as they plunged deeper into the forest.

Morales dared to look up, wondering how far they could possibly go before they broke apart or came to a halt. He raised his head just in time to see a section of mast sweeping toward him. He ducked too late. Pain like hot fire erupted in his skull.

And then all was black.

"I told you this was the work of the devil." Dominic scowled out the window at the dense foliage of the swamp into which *San Amaro* had come to rest. "This place is nothing but a haven for foul creatures, both great and small. Biting, stinging, and worse."

"We lived through that storm. That is the work of God." Three days later Morales still felt the effects of the blow to the head he had suffered. He'd spent little time outside of his cabin, just enough to remind the crew that he was still alive and in command. Too much exertion made him feel faint, and it would not do to show weakness in front of a crew that stood on the verge of desperation.

He'd managed to keep the men busy with hunting, gathering, and scouting. They couldn't range far. The storm had turned this swamp into one giant pool of quicksand. *Already San Amaro* was sinking into the soft earth. He prayed the ship would hold together, as she provided their sole protection from the elements.

"What are we going to do, Captain?" Dominic's dull voice struck a note of fatalism. "We're trapped in this quagmire."

"The weather is hale. Eventually, the swamp will become passable and we will make our way to shore. From there we will find our way to an outpost. La Florida is filled with game and fruit. We should have no trouble keeping ourselves fed during the journey."

"That is not what I meant." Dominic turned to face him, his face wan. "There is something out there, many somethings if our scouts are correct. The men have never seen the like before."

"Superstitious nonsense." Morales waved his first mate's comment away. "The men had a great fright, and they are temporarily trapped in a forbidding environment. It is only natural that their minds begin to deceive them."

Dominic hesitated. "Manuel is hardly a superstitious man. He is the oldest and most experienced of them all and he says he has seen demons in the swamp."

"All sailors are superstitious, and the fact that he claims to have seen demons proves it. Besides, I seem to recall Manuel insisting he once made love to a mermaid." He would have said more, but shouts from the direction of the crew deck drew his attention. "What is going on out there?"

"I'll see." Dominic hurried out of the cabin and returned ten minutes later with a grave look on his face. "You must come and see this."

"What is it?" The look on his mate's face gave Morales an uneasy feeling.

"You have to see it for yourself."

Morales eased himself up off the bed and paused to let the wave of dizziness pass. Slowly, taking great care to stand up straight, he made his way to the crew deck.

The men were huddled around a sand fire pit they'd made in the center of the deck. The scents of acrid smoke, roasting meat, and coppery blood greeted Morales as he approached the excited men. He lacked the strength to force his way through the crowd, so he merely stood there, leaning against the wall in what he hoped was a casual manner, until the men became aware of his presence. Silence rippled through the group as, one by one, the men spotted the captain. Not one man met his gaze.

"We didn't do it, Captain," one of the younger men, Alonso, muttered. "We came back from patrol and found...that." He pointed at the fire pit.

Summoning all his reserves of energy, Morales made his slow way forward. The sailors parted like the Red Sea to Moses as the captain approached the fire pit, until only one man stood in his path.

"We needed meat," Manuel, the veteran sailor said.

"And what sort of meat have you brought us?" Morales stepped around Manuel and froze. Even stripped of skin, he could recognize human arms and legs roasting in the fire. "Cannibalism!" He drew his sword in a flash and pressed the tip to Manuel's throat. "I'll flay you alive for this. Whose body is this? Who have you killed?"

"You misunderstand," Manuel gasped, his eyes locked on the gleaming blade of Morales' sword. "It's one of the creatures we've been seeing. I thought they were demons, but they're actually some sort of ape. One of them attacked me with a stone club and I ran it through."

"An ape? In La Florida?"

"Someone show him." Manuel said.

One of the crewmen picked something up off the deck and held it up for the captain to see. Morales' jaw and sword arm dropped in unison as his eyes fell on the horrific sight.

"What in God's name is it?" That thing, whatever it was, was no ape.

No one had time to answer, because angry howls coming from outside the ship split the air, echoing down into the crew deck. Something heavy thudded against the ship and Morales flinched. What was happening?

"Manuel. Get up on the main deck and see what's happening."

The sailors exchanged dark looks but no one aside from Manuel made a move. They all waited in tense silence until the sailor returned.

"I can't see anything through the trees, but the sounds are coming from all around." He swallowed hard. "I think it's the...apes... or whatever they are. They have us surrounded."

"How many do you think there are?"

"I can't say for certain. Ten? Twenty?" Manuel began

to tremble. "I didn't mean to anger them. I was only defending myself."

"If the situation was reversed, and it was one of our own killed by these...apes, would that matter to you?"

Manuel hung his head.

"It doesn't matter," Morales said. "You had no choice. You couldn't let yourself be killed. We need you." He looked around at his men, all wide-eyed and various shades of pale. "We must be prepared to defend ourselves, should it prove necessary. Dominic, set a guard." The mate nodded.

Morales turned his eyes to the fire pit and the disturbingly human-looking meat that cooked there. "You might as well eat. We're going to need our strength."

He headed for his cabin, unable to watch the men devour their unsavory meal.

"Madre de Dios," he whispered. "The monsters are real."

CHAPTER 1

Miami, Florida

It was a bar like any other. Loud music and even louder conversation competed to drown out the baseball game showing on the televisions hanging from the walls. Bones selected a table in the corner, ordered up hot wings and a bottle of Dos Equis, and sat back to watch the door. This was his kind of place. The only thing missing, he thought, was the stale smell of cigarette smoke, but that had been absent since banning smoking in public places had become a thing. Bones didn't care for cigarettes, but there was something about the musty aroma that made the atmosphere in this sort of place just right.

He didn't have to wait long. He was just digging into his chicken wings when a slender, dark-haired woman came in through the door. She spotted him immediately, smiled, and made her way across the room. As she passed, several sets of eyes followed her progress. Bones couldn't blame them. The woman moved with confidence and grace. Of course, most of the men were probably admiring the way she filled out her form–fitting clothing. She had just the right amount of curves to balance out her athletic build and she tossed her long, brown hair in just the right way. She was a looker, no doubt.

"Mister Bonebrake, she said, reaching out to shake his hand. "I'm Joanna Slater. You can call me Jo or Slater, whichever you prefer."

"You can call me Bones. I don't answer to anything

else unless I'm at a family reunion."

"Fair enough." Slater slid gracefully into her seat and signaled for the waiter, who was already on his way over.

"I would've ordered you a round, but I don't know what you like to drink."

"I'll drink just about anything if someone else is buying." She turned to the waiter. "I'll take one of what he's having, and go ahead and bring us another round."

"You're off to a good start," Bones said, nodding in approval. "So, tell me what I can do for you. I assume it has something to do with your television show." Bones knew that Slater hosted *Expedition Adventure,* a cable television show that focused on ancient mysteries and cryptids—mysterious creatures whose existence had not yet been documented by science. "You're in Florida, so what are we talking here? The Fountain of Youth?"

Slater smiled. "So you're already familiar with my show? I'm flattered."

"I never miss an episode. I'm interested in the subject matter, and you're not nearly as full of crap as some of the other hosts of programs like yours. The guy with the wild hair? Total nutbag." Bones said.

Slater laughed. "Let's not name any names, but I know exactly what you mean." Just then, the waiter arrived with their drinks. "Good service here."

"I thing beautiful women get good service here. He wasn't nearly that fast when I did the ordering."

Slater arched an eyebrow. "Do you really think I'm beautiful or are you just hitting on me?"

"A little bit of both, but business before pleasure." He took a long drink, enjoying the rich flavor and the tangy zing of lime.

Slater took a drink, set her bottle down, and then leveled her gaze at Bones. "I'm investigating the skunk ape."

Bones closed his eyes and shook his head. "Seriously? Dude, I can point you to half a dozen legends that are more worthy of investigation than that thing."

Also known as the swamp ape, Florida Bigfoot, and swampsquatch, among other names, the skunk ape was a primate cryptid reputed to reside in the southeastern United States. Though sightings ranged throughout the South, from North Carolina all the way to Arkansas, the creature was most commonly identified with southern Florida, where nearly all the alleged sightings had occurred.

"You don't think there's at least a story worth investigating? You weren't always such a skeptic." Slater opened a portfolio, drew out a sheet of paper, and slid it across the table. She had printed out a screen capture from an Internet forum. Bones recognized it immediately.

"Look at the date on that post. I made it years ago. I didn't know crap back then."

Slater was undeterred. "You believed it at the time. What changed?"

"I did a little investigating. There's no solid evidence, just some crappy video of drunk college kids in monkey suits and a few misidentifications of black bears."

"There's a lot more than that," Slater said. "I've investigated my share of cryptid reports and some of these witnesses seem reliable to me. They describe the way it looked, sounded, even the way it smelled."

"And if any of them had spent much time in the

woods they'd have recognized that smell for what it probably was — a bobcat." He held up a hand, forestalling her next argument. "I've also seen the plaster casts of supposed skunk ape tracks. They're all fake. You've done Bigfoot investigations so you know the telltale signs."

Slater sighed. "I can see you're going to be a hard sell. You are correct. I *do* know the telltale signs of falsified primate tracks, which is why I believe these are genuine." She took out a stack of glossy, 8 x 10 photographs and handed them to Bones. "I haven't had the chance to examine them up close yet, but from what I can tell, they look like the real thing."

Bones could see what she meant. Most of the castings that were made of primate footprints, at least of the cryptozoological kind, were too regular, too even. These were different. They were deeper in some places, reflecting the way a primate's weight distribution shifted as it walked and the way it bore more weight on the big toe than on the others. He couldn't deny he was impressed. What's more, he had, in his time, personally confirmed the existence of a few so-called cryptids, though he kept that information to himself.

"Not bad," he admitted, handing the photographs back to Slater. "Where did you get these?"

"From an investigator who lives south of Sarasota. You know, the area where the Myakka photographs were taken?" Slater smiled, her brown eyes twinkling. She seemed to think she had Bones hooked.

"You mean the anonymous photographs of an orangutan? Even if they're legit, all it proves is someone's pet got loose."

"And if that's what the investigation turns up, that's fine by me. The Everglades is home to plenty of non-native species: exotic birds, escaped pet snakes that grow to giant size, and more. I think our viewers would be fascinated by the idea of an orangutan, or even a troop of them, surviving and maybe even thriving in the Florida swamps."

Bones nodded. He couldn't deny the woman was persuasive but he still wasn't completely buying it. "Why did you reach out to me?" he asked, changing the subject.

"We found you through that message board post. My staff tracked you down and vetted you. There's surprisingly little information about you out there."

"No comment." Bones took a long drink and let Slater continue.

"Anyway, we learned enough about you to determine that you have interest in, and knowledge of, cryptids. Also, nothing we found raised any red flags, meaning you're not a total whack job." She hesitated, blushed, and took a drink. "Also, you would look... impressive on camera."

"So my porn career never came up?" Bones laughed as Slater's eyes went wide and her jaw dropped. "Just kidding." He took another drink just to keep her in suspense, and then smiled. "All right, you've piqued my interest. What's the pay?"

CHAPTER 2

Sarasota, Florida

The offices of the Sarasota Sun stood on the corner of
Ringling Boulevard and South Osprey Avenue in the
heart of town. Bones squeezed his Dodge Ram pickup
truck into a narrow parking space, cranked up some
AC/DC on the stereo, and waited for Slater to arrive. He
hadn't been there long when a sharp rap on his tailgate
startled him. He glanced in the rearview mirror and saw
a man in the all-black uniform of the Sarasota County
Sheriff's Department beckoning to him.

Bones rolled down his window and stuck his head
out. "What can I do for you, officer?"

"It's deputy, and you can start by shutting off that
vehicle and getting your narrow behind out here where I
can talk to you." Though his ruddy features and sturdy
build didn't scream "inbreeder", the man's southern
drawl marked him as a likely member of one of the long-
term native families rather than a more recent transplant
from somewhere up north. He was probably a redneck.
Bones hated rednecks.

Slowly, he cut the engine, opened the door, and slid
out into the tight space between his truck and the vehicle
alongside him.

"I don't know how they do things down in Munro
County," the deputy said, glancing at Bones' license
plate, "but around here, when an officer of the law gives
you an order you obey it without..." He halted in
midsentence as Bones stepped out from between the

vehicles. The deputy was not a small man. He was a shade over six feet tall and solidly built, and probably accustomed to physically intimidating most of the people he encountered, but next to the broad shouldered, six foot five Cherokee, he was a bit on the small side.

"Sorry about the delay," Bones lied, trying to make his smile as friendly as possible, "Deputy Logan," he added after a glance at the man's name tag. He said nothing else. He knew he done nothing wrong so he simply waited for the deputy to explain himself.

"You know why I called you out here?" The deputy had regained some of his fire, but his demeanor was decidedly less pugnacious than it had been a moment before.

"If it's to tell me how freaking hot and humid it is in this town, I've already noticed."

The deputy didn't crack a smile. "You mind telling me what you doing sitting here?"

"Listening to music. Good old classic rock. You into that stuff?"

"Excuse me?" The deputy shuffled his feet as if debating whether or not to take a step toward Bones.

"Am I free to go?" Bones knew he probably shouldn't mess with the man, but he didn't appreciate being rousted for no particular reason. "Or am I under arrest?"

"I just want to know what you're doing here. You're from down south, which is a pipeline for the drug trade, and you're sitting here in this parking lot doing nothing."

"He's waiting for me." Slater had arrived. She strolled up to the deputy and flashed an apologetic smile. "He and I have an appointment with someone inside." She inclined her head toward the newspaper office. "I'm running late. Please accept my apology."

The deputy looked like he had just sucked a lemon. He looked from Bones to Slater and then nodded. "All right. Just don't loiter in the parking lot when you're done." He didn't wait for a reply but turned and stalked back to his car, climbed in, and drove away.

When the deputy was gone, Slater turned and frowned at Bones. "Do you always treat people like that?"

Bones shook his head. "Nope, but bullies and rednecks get on my nerves."

"I don't know how many of the former we will encounter but we're likely to meet up with plenty of the latter. Do you think you can keep your attitude in check?"

"You're the boss." Bones looked up and squinted at the late morning sun. "What do you say we blow this appointment off and head over to the Siesta Key Oyster Bar? I hear it's a great place to hang out and pound a few brews."

"When this investigation is finished I'll let you buy me a pitcher, but not until the work is done."

"Bummer. I thought you were a party girl."

Slater rolled her eyes and led the way into the office.

The reporter who greeted them was a weedy, bespectacled man with a rat face and a thatch of yellow hair. He barely glanced at Bones, having eyes only for Slater. Bones couldn't blame the man. She was garbed in a tight tank top, snug fitting khaki shorts, and hiking boots. With her brown hair hanging in a braid down the middle of her back, she was giving off a serious Lara Croft vibe. Bones couldn't deny the look worked for her.

"I'm Gage," the reporter said. "Please follow me." He led them to a tiny cubicle in the far corner of the building, and sat down in front of a cluttered desk lined with bobble head dolls of famous baseball players. When bones and Slater had pulled up chairs and sat down, Gage got down to business.

"I understand you are interested in the skunk ape." He kept his voice low, frequently glancing about as if spies lurked in every corner.

"That's right," Slater said. "I host a television show and we're doing a feature on it. I understand you are the man to speak to on the subject."

The compliment did the trick. Gage relaxed and a smile spread across his face. "I'm a local affairs reporter, so the skunk ape is strictly a hobby. I have, however, done extensive research." He took out an overstuffed accordion folder and handed it to Slater. "This is all of the information I've gathered: newspaper clippings, articles from the web, transcripts of eyewitness reports including interviews I personally conducted, research into possible scientific explanations, and a summary of my conclusions in the back."

"This is wonderful," Slater said. "Is there somewhere we can sit and examine it?"

"These are copies," Gage said. "I only ask that you credit me if you use any of the material in your show."

"You've gone to a lot of trouble. Thank you."

"If it will help you prove that the skunk ape is real, or at least its existence is a real possibility, it will have been more than worth the effort." He looked around again. "I don't mind telling you that people around here give me a hard time about my research."

"I know what you mean," Bones said. "I'm into cryptids, alien visitor theories, and all that kind of stuff. Most people don't get it."

Gage nodded. "Yes, but it's not just that. In general, the locals don't like it when anyone talks about the skunk ape. The transplants from other parts of the country are concerned about our community's image. They think treating the legends seriously makes us look like a bunch of hicks. The families who have lived in the community for generations are afraid Sarasota is going to, I don't know, turn into Roswell, New Mexico. You know, drawing in the oddballs and pseudo-scientists. Sorry," he said, blushing, "but you know what I mean."

Bones and Slater nodded in unison.

"I'm just saying," Gage continued, "don't be surprised if you get a lot of push-back. And be careful where you go and who you talk to."

CHAPTER 3

Gage snapped his head around as a long shadow ran across his keyboard. He looked up to see a tall man in a sheriff's department uniform standing over him, arms folded.

"How can I help you, Deputy Logan?" He couldn't stand the man. He was a scion, if someone who lived in rundown mobile home on the edge of the swamp could properly bear that title, of a long-time local family. As such, the deputy stuck his nose into everyone's business and had an opinion on how just about everything should be done.

"You had some visitors today." It wasn't a question.

Gage gritted his teeth. Damn Logan and his reticence. "Would you care to explain why you're investigating my activities?"

Gage threw back his head and laughed. "Don't get your panties in a bunch, Gay," he said, using the high school nickname Logan and his football buddies had slapped onto Gage so many years ago. "I happened to be in the office and saw some unfamiliar faces, and I wondered who they were and what they were up to. I mean, why would outsiders need to meet with a local affairs reporter?"

"I'm afraid that's confidential," Gage said through gritted teeth. He felt his cheeks begin to heat. He hated Logan and despised the way the man could get a reaction out of him with such ease. Sometimes it didn't get better after high school.

Logan smiled and sat down on the corner of Gage's

desk. "You got this all wrong. I'm just looking out for my town, same as always. I'm not trying to get on your nerves or anything.

"Well, you have. Same as always."

"Look, you know I care about this town and the people who live in it, even the fellows who are still mad about a wedgie twenty years ago." He grinned. "Truth is, there was an incident outside with that big Indian fellow. It didn't amount to nothing, but something ain't right about him. He's from down south and we know what kind of characters come from there. I ran his plate, so I already know his name." He leaned in and laid a heavy hand on Gage's shoulder. "I'm just asking you, as an old high school buddy, to give me an idea of what the man's up to. No details, nothing personal. Just the big picture."

Gage bit his jaw, holding back a profane retort. He knew Logan would keep pestering him until he got what he wanted.

"By the way," Logan said, letting go of Gage's shoulder and sitting back, "we're starting afternoon rush hour patrols on your street. I'll tell the boys to keep an eye out for your car."

The implication was clear. If Gage played ball, the deputies would leave him alone. If not, he doubtless would be pulled over for some nonexistent violation. Besides, given that Gage's interest in the skunk ape was well-known, he figured Logan had already put two and two together. The deputy was a buffoon but he wasn't a complete idiot. Despising himself for giving in so easily, he sat up and looked Logan in the eye.

"It's nothing serious. They're from one of those pseudo-investigative television shows and they're doing an episode about the skunk ape."

Logan guffawed and slapped his thigh. "So that fellow *is* crazy. I knew he wasn't right, but at least it isn't drugs. I should have known, since the skunk ape is sort of your thing. What did you tell him?"

"Just the usual stuff. Nothing they couldn't find on the internet."

"You didn't tell them it's all a big fake?"

Gage scowled. "You know I don't believe that."

Logan slid down off the desk. "No, you don't, do you? All right, Gay, I'll tell the fellows to let the ace reporter in the yellow Volkswagen pass unmolested."

I'll just bet you will, Gage thought as he watched the deputy walk away. He considered calling Slater to warn her about the meddling deputy, but decided he didn't need to be involved any more deeply than he already was.

"I've done my part," he mumbled, "and good luck to you."

CHAPTER 4

Slater had left her car behind and walked from her hotel to the newspaper office, so she rode along with Bones as they headed to their next appointment. He was pleased to find they shared similar taste in music, though she did request the Black Eyed Peas, which he told her in no uncertain terms was not on his phone. "They can't decide if they are rock or rap, and they suck at both," he explained.

"Just when I was starting to respect your opinion," Slater said, shaking her head.

"So, who is this guy we're paying a visit to?" He asked, struggling to keep his eyes trained on the road and not on Slater's legs.

"Nigel Gambles. He's the cryptozoologist who made the plaster castings of the alleged skunk ape tracks. He lives in a cabin near the entrance to the Myakka River State Park. My crew will meet us there."

Slater's crew turned out to be a two-person team: a short, skinny young woman named Carly, and a round-faced, thickset man named Dave. The two hurried over when Bones and Slater got out of the truck.

"I'm the cameraman," Dave said, unnecessarily holding up his camera, "and Carly is the sound engineer."

"I'm Bones. I don't think I have a title."

"Of course you do. You're the resident expert." Carly grinned and gave him a tiny wink which he returned. She was cute—not Slater-level, but not bad.

"I'm not paying any of you to flirt," Slater said. "Let's go. Mister Gambles is expecting us."

Gambles' cabin stood at the end of a long, winding dirt driveway lined by live oaks and draped by low-hanging Spanish moss. The deep shade did little to dull the Florida heat, but any respite was welcome to Bones, who had ditched his trademark leather jacket but kept his jeans. Shorts weren't his thing unless he was going to the gym or for a run.

Gambles was a trim man with close-cropped hair and friendly eyes. He spoke with a slight accent, but Bones wasn't familiar enough with the various regional forms to say from where in Britain the man hailed. London, perhaps? Gambles invited them in and immediately set to talking about his most recent discovery, but Slater gently interrupted him.

"We really want to hear everything you have to say, but let's get it recorded so you don't have to cover anything twice, okay?"

Gambles agreed, and when Dave and Carly had everything in place, he took up a position in front of a bookcase laden with titles relating to cryptozoology. Slater sat down in a chair facing him and began an Oprah-style interview.

"Can you tell us about the skunk ape?"

Gambles nodded. "The skunk ape is a legendary primate that is believed to inhabit the Everglades and outlying areas, though sightings have been reported all around Florida and in other states in the Southeast. It's known for its elusiveness and its distinctive smell."

He went on to discuss the history of skunk ape sightings in the area, beginning with Native American legends and reports from Spanish explorers, including a harrowing tale of a shipwrecked crew, of whom all but one were killed by the legendary beasts. He then moved along to modern sightings, skirting around the obvious fakes, but providing multiple accounts from ostensibly reliable witnesses, and even sharing a few grainy photographs. Bones had seen and heard it all before, but what Gambles said next surprised him.

"Some people believe that the creature is not an ape, but a primitive human."

Bones almost spoke up, but remembered the camera was rolling, and kept his silence. Slater, however, followed up.

"Primitive humans? Is there any evidence to support this theory?"

"In truth, there's not much evidence to support *any* theory, but I have found what I believe are rudimentary tools and stones that show signs of being worked. What's more, I discovered them in the general area where I recently came across the tracks."

Gambles picked up the briefcase sitting beside his chair, opened it, and took out a palm-sized stone. "This looks like a scraping tool." He held it up for the camera and then handed it to Slater, who examined it with polite interest. "And this one," he continued, taking out a triangular stone, "appears to be for cutting. See how the edges have been chipped away? It's not a regular break. Someone or something has worked it."

The man wasn't wrong. Even from where he stood, Bones could tell that someone had scraped and chipped the rock to give it a sharp edge. Slater seemed to agree, nodding slowly as she looked it over. "But how do we know these aren't artifacts from the Native Americans who once lived in this area?"

"Because I have evidence that at least one item was used quite recently." Gambles took out a smooth, round stone about the size of a tennis ball and a Ziploc bag containing small, gray fragments of some unrecognizable material. "It appears this stone was used to break open freshwater clams."

Slater frowned. "Why would someone smash them instead of just prying them open? It ruins the meat."

"Exactly!" Gambles sat up straighter as he spoke, a triumphant smile playing across his face. "You or I would do just that. But what if you did not have a knife or other implement at your disposal? Or what if you didn't know such things existed? Only a true primitive would use a bludgeoning tool for this sort of work."

Slater adopted a properly interested expression, paused for a few moments to let viewers appreciate the implications, and then continued with the questions.

"Tell us about the other evidence you've recently uncovered."

This was clearly the moment Gambles had been waiting for. He leaned forward, his words coming faster. "I was taking a stroll down by the river and the tracks were just there. My first thought was that someone was winding me up."

"Why would you think that?" Slater asked.

"My neighbors know I'm a cryptozoologist. Truth told, they think I'm a bit of a nutter so I thought one of them might be having some fun at my expense. Then I realized that I was well off my usual route. No one would have any reason to believe I'd have gone so deep into the swamp. If someone wanted to play a joke on me, they'd have planted the tracks somewhere I'd be sure to stumble across them."

"Of course, that doesn't mean the tracks aren't fake—only that they probably weren't intended specifically for you," Slater pointed out. Bones was impressed that she didn't merely accept the man's story at face value. "What makes you believe these tracks are genuine?"

"That's a fair question." Gambles once again reached into his briefcase, this time taking out a set of photographs. He passed most of them to Slater, but kept one which he held up for the benefit of the camera. "I immediately took some photographs with my cellphone, just in case someone or something disturbed the tracks before I could return. I then hurried home to retrieve my camera and my footprint kit. These are the high-resolution images I took. You can see they bear some resemblance to ape footprints, but are also reminiscent of very old tracks found in Africa." He handed the last photograph to Slater.

"Finally, there are the castings I made of the prints." He carefully removed two bubble-wrapped objects from the briefcase, closed the case, and set it on the floor. "The prints do not show the telltale signs of fakery." He went on to describe the same details Slater and Bones had discussed at the bar.

When Gambles finished his analysis of the print castings, Slater asked a final question.

"Do you believe the skunk ape is real and lives in this area?"

Gambles looked directly into the camera and gave a firm nod.

"Absolutely."

CHAPTER 5

They parked in a gravel lot just inside the Myakka River State Park and hiked from there, following a walking trail south along the river bank until it ended. After that, they relied on Gambles' directions and a topographical map he had provided. Bones had plenty of experience with this sort of thing so they had little trouble making their way to the spot the researcher had described — a place where a rutted dirt road, little used, met the river.

Here, the Myakka River made a sharp bend. A sandy shoal protruded out into it, and a mud bank lay on the other side of the water, rising in a gentle slope up to the dense forest beyond. Birdsong and the gentle rush of the river filled Bones' ears. He could almost forget they were only a few miles from civilization.

"Do you think this is the right spot?" Slater asked, looking around.

"This is definitely it." He pointed to the location on the topographical map where the winding blue ribbon of the Myakka formed a loop. "Here's where we are on the map. It matches perfectly."

"In that case, let's get started." Slater took up a position near the water's edge and waited for Dave and Carly to get their equipment ready. Dave had left his large camera locked in the trunk of his car and was now using a small, handheld video recorder, while Carly opted for a portable digital recorder.

When Dave gave Slater the thumbs-up she recorded a brief segment, introducing this as the spot where Gambles had found the skunk ape tracks and describing the setting. Once the recording was finished, they began a search of the area.

While the others scoured the shoals and the bank on their side of the river, Bones waded across to inspect the opposite side. The water was shallow, little more than ankle–deep, and it felt cool and refreshing on his bare feet. When he was halfway across, he turned and called back to Slater.

"What do you say we let those two keep looking around while you and I do a little skinny dipping?"

"Keep dreaming." Slater didn't even look up from her searching.

"Maybe later then." Bones turned around and froze. Even at a distance of twenty feet or more he could clearly make out a set of long-toed footprints on the mud bank. At first glance they appeared to be the twin of those Gambles had found.

"No way. Hey, Slater, get over here!" He turned and beckoned to her.

"Give it a rest. I'm trying to work here and I don't have time to..."

"I found a track."

"Really?" Slater looked in the direction he pointed and her jaw dropped. "Fantastic! Dave, get over..." She paused and cocked her head to the side. "What's that noise?"

From somewhere in the distance came the low rumble of an engine, growing louder as it drew near. Moments later, a monster truck bounded into view, bouncing on its raised suspension as its oversized tires rolled through the ruts of the overgrown dirt road. Dave and Carly leaped to the side as the truck shot down the bank, fishtailed on the sand, and sped into the water. It roared past Bones, drenching him in cold river water.

Bones cursed and sprang back. He shook the water out of his eyes just in time to see the truck rumble of the mud bank, lose traction, and slide backward.

Right over the footprints.

"Are you freaking kidding me?" he yelled. He stomped toward the truck, but the driver threw the vehicle into reverse and back straight at him, forcing Bones to spring out of the way again. The driver did a donut, churning up a wall of water that wash the mud bank clean and sprayed Bones with another cold, wet wave. The truck shot back across the river toward the old dirt road but skidded to a halt in the sand when Slater ran directly into its path.

"What the hell do you idiots think you are doing?" she screamed. "You almost killed three of my people."

The doors opened and two men stepped out of the truck. The driver was bald with a bushy red beard and a bowling ball body. The passenger was a tall, brown-haired man with a rat tail and several gaps in his teeth.

"You got a problem, girl?" Rat Tail folded his sinewy arms and spat a wad of phlegm on the sand.

Slater didn't give an inch. She stood with her hands on her hips and fire in her eyes, staring daggers up at the taller men. "I just told you what my problem is. Are you deaf or just stupid?"

"I didn't expect no sass from a girl as pretty as you," Rat Tail cackled. "Maybe for Miss Short-haired Lesbian over there." He inclined his head toward Carly, who held out her hands, frowned, and mouthed, *I'm not gay.*

Slater trembled with rage. "We're conducting

research here and you morons just screwed it up. I've got half a mind to sue you. I hope your mom's double-wide is worth something, or else we'll have to take your neon beer sign and your NASCAR memorabilia."

"This one's got a mouth on her," Bowling Ball observed. "I think somebody should shut it."

"I can't tell you how much I'd love to see you try." Bones said, stepping up behind the men and giving each a shove in the back. He didn't put much force into the effort — just enough to divert their attention from Slater.

The two men rounded on him in unison but hesitated when their eyes fell on him. Bowling Ball was as broad of shoulder as Bones and Rat Tail nearly as tall, but neither had his combination of height and breadth. This, however, did not stymie them in the least. They exchanged grins.

"Well, it looks like it's going to be a good day after all," bowling ball said. "You see, we came here to drink beer and..."

"I know, I know. Drink some beer and kick some ass and you're almost out of beer. Dude, do you know how old that movie is? Come up with some new material or go back to kissing your boyfriend."

The man frowned, trying to process the insult.

"You know, you talk pretty big for a man who's outnumbered two to one, Indian Boy," Rat Tail said.

"I'm surprised you can count that high," Bones said. "I guess that second grade education was good for something after all."

"And it's not two to one. It'll be two on two." Dave handed his camera to Carly and made to join Bones.

"Thanks, Bro, but it's not your fight. How about you

get the girls out of here?"

Dave hesitated. Bones could tell the young cameraman was struggling between a sense of duty and the natural aversion to of violence common in most people. Normal people, that was. But Bones was hardly normal.

"Seriously, dude. You don't need to watch this and neither do they."

Bowling Ball chuckled. "You don't want your little girlfriend to see you get your ass kicked?" he taunted as he and Rat Tail advanced shoulder-to-shoulder.

Bones looked the man in the eye and smiled. "Not exactly."

He lashed out with a vicious sidekick that caught Rat Tail in the gut. Taken by surprise, the tall man folded forward and crumbled to his knees. He knelt there, arms pressed to his stomach, struggling to catch his breath.

Bowling Ball's reaction time was better than that of his friend. He swung a wild haymaker at Bones' head. Bones moved back just enough for the blow to miss his chin by half an inch, and then he drove his fist into the exposed temple of his off-balance opponent. Bowling Ball wobbled backward. Bones followed with a knee to the man's groin, a blow which sent him to the ground, and then a roundhouse kick to his head that turned out his lights.

He turned on Rat Tail, who had regained his feet and was charging at Bones. Rat Tail lowered his head and tried a tackle, but he wasn't strong enough to bring the larger man down. Bones flung him to the ground, jumped onto his back, and caught him in a chokehold. Rat Tail struggled and clawed at Bones' forearm, which was locked around his neck in a Python grip, but his efforts were futile and he soon went limp. Bones let the man fall to the ground.

"He's not dead is he?" Carly asked.

Bones shook his head. "Just unconscious." He strode over to the still idling truck, took the keys from the ignition, and pitched them into the river. He then searched the glove compartment and found a 38 revolver. He emptied the cylinder, tossed the bullets into the water, and put the weapon back where he'd found it.

"Come on," he said to the others. "Let's get out of here before these idiots wake up. If I have to deal with them again I might bruise my knuckles."

Dave chuckled. "That was crazy. You took them out in, like, thirty seconds."

"It only took that long because I decided to choke the dude out." He looked down at Dave. "It's not like the movies. A real fight is short and nasty and somebody almost always gets hurt. That's why you should try to stay out of them if at all possible." He turned and walked back out into the river.

"Where are you going?" Slater asked. "They destroyed the prints."

"Were going to do this old-school. Something left those prints and I'm going to track it down."

CHAPTER 6

Bones was an experienced tracker and he was able to follow the signs left by the passage of whatever had passed this way with little trouble. The ground was thick with undergrowth, but here and there he spotted a partial footprint, broken branch, or a twig or leaf pressed down into the soft earth. The first couple of times he spotted something, Slater had him point it out and explain it for the benefit of the camera, but after that they moved on as quickly as they could.

The path they followed, if it could be called that, plunged deep into the swampy forest, occasionally bending back in the direction of the river, but generally following a southeasterly course. Bones lost the trail a couple of times and was forced to double back again, but always managed to find it. The farther they went, the quieter their surroundings grew. It was hard to believe they were only a handful of miles from a decent-sized city.

Spirits were high during the first hour or so of their trek. The crew was duly impressed by his tracking skills and never voiced any concerns that he might be steering them on the wrong course. By the second hour, though, their enthusiasm began to wane.

"Is it dangerous here?" Dave asked. "I mean, aside from crazy rednecks?"

"It can be if you're not careful. While we're in the woods, you're not likely to run into anything. I guess there's an outside chance we could stumble across a black bear, but the odds of one of them messing with us are pretty slim. They just want to be left alone. If we do see one, just follow my lead and it'll be cool."

"You said 'while we're in the woods.' What about when we get to the swamp?" Dave smiled as he spoke, but Bones could hear a tremble in his voice.

"Snakes and gators, but just keep your eyes open and you should be fine. And try to stay out of the water. I don't want to have to pull you out of quicksand."

"I hear there are giant pythons in the swamp," Carly said. "People buy them as pets and set them free when they grow too big."

Bones donned his most patient smile. "Tell you what. You guys take a break from worrying and stay close to me. It'll be fine."

"How far are we going to go?" Carly asked, glancing back the way they'd come.

"Until we find something, I guess," Bones said. "Or until the boss tells us it's time to knock off for the day."

"It's still early," Slater said. "Plenty of daylight left."

Carly didn't seem pleased. "Are you sure we'll be able to find our way back?"

"I'm sure *I* can get us back. All I have to do is follow the tracks you three have trampled into the ground. Seriously, it's like an elephant walk back there."

"What if we get separated from you?" Dave chimed in, unabashed by Bones' commentary on his woodcraft.

"Don't." Bones turned away and resumed his trek, but Dave wasn't satisfied.

"No, really. What do we do if we get lost?"

Bones stopped and counted to three before replying. "Seriously? The kind of show you do and you've never spent any time out in the woods?"

"Not in such a small group, and not with a guide who can follow invisible trails through the middle of nowhere. Besides, this place is..."

"...creepy," Carly finished.

Bones shrugged out of his backpack, took out a bottle of water, and took a long drink, buying time for his annoyance to subside. "All right. Listen carefully. If one of you wanders off, head east until you hit the river and then turn right. Follow it until you get back to the park. It's really that simple." He supposed he should explain to them how to determine which way was east. "To know which direction is east, you just..."

"It's cool," Dave said. "Our cell phones have compass apps." His countenance suddenly brightened. "Wait a minute!" He took out his phone and tapped it a few times. "I've got a signal. That means I can use GPS to get back. Looks like there was nothing to worry about."

Bones pressed his lips tightly together until he could speak without cursing. "That's just...awesome." Not trusting himself to say more, he turned on his heel and plunged forward, double-time.

Bones continued to follow the signs left by whatever had passed this way. The occasional partial print kept his spirits up. These were no shoe or boot prints. They were tracks left by large, bare feet. He was finally beginning to consider the possibility that the skunk ape was, in fact, a reality and not a mere legend. Of course, he was predisposed to wish that such things were true, but that didn't change what he saw as he moved through the forest. Tracks were immune to personal bias.

"Do you think we might actually find something?"

Carly's tone indicated she wasn't exactly thrilled by the possibility.

"I hope so," Bones said, keeping his eyes on the ground in front of him.

"What if we come across an actual skunk ape?" Dave asked.

"No offense, but as clumsy as you white people are out here in the woods, any woodland creature worth its salt is going to hear you coming a mile away and clear the hell out of the area until we're gone."

"Somebody's snippy today," Slater said.

"Sorry. I get that way when I concentrate. It hurts my brain to think too hard." He grinned at his three companions, hoping to break the ice a little.

"We'll try to be quiet, won't we, guys?" Slater glared at her crew, who nodded in unison.

Bones knew it wouldn't do much good. None of them were practiced at woodcraft, but at least they were making an effort. He supposed he might as well give them some pointers.

"A few things to keep in mind. First of all, don't step on anything that will make noise, like twigs, dry leaves, or loose stones. Try to step where I step."

"Because we're all seven feet tall." Slater gave him a wink.

"Just do your best. Also, try not to brush against anything. That makes unnecessary noise. Ideally, the only thing you'll touch out here is soft earth with the balls of your feet. And try not to talk so much. Got it?"

"It ain't going to help." A new voice rang out from somewhere up ahead, amused, with a touch of youthfulness. A young man, freckled and sandy-haired, stepped out from behind a live oak. He wore overalls with no shirt underneath and carried a .22 rifle. Bones put him at about thirteen years old, give or take a year. "Either you're a woodsman or you ain't." The boy cleared his throat and spat on the ground. "You are," he nodded at Bones, "but they ain't."

"They're trying," Bones said. "You live around here?"

The boy shrugged. "Not real close by, but I spend a lot of time out here."

"What's the gun for?"

"Squirrels or whatever else I might feel like having for dinner."

Bones nodded. He enjoyed squirrel meat from time to time, though he had to go home to North Carolina to get any. "You got a name?"

"Yep." The boy's face cracked into a wide smile and his eyes sparkled. He seemed to think he'd made a great joke.

Rednecks, Bones thought. *I can't even stand the juvenile of the species.* "I'm Bones; this is Slater, Carly, and Dave."

"I'm Jack."

"You said you spend a lot of time in these woods?" Bones asked.

The boy raised his eyebrows. "Is Danica Patrick a race car driver?"

"I have no freaking idea."

"She is and she ain't. She drives a race car but she's a woman so she ain't no race car driver." The boy threw back his head and cackled.

"Youthful misogyny," Slater mumbled, "such a sight to behold in its nascence."

"I actually understood that," Bones said. He turned back to Jack. "We're tracking something," he said. "Something that moves on two feet. You haven't seen anything unusual, have you?"

The boy froze, his eyes suddenly hard and his expression blank. "That ain't a good idea. You should just go on back where you came from."

"Can't do it. You got any idea which way we should go? I'm going to find the trail one way or the other, but it would save me some time if you'd point me in the right direction."

"There's twenty bucks in it for you," Slater said.

Jack spat on the ground again. "Thank you, but I shouldn't take your money. If you're hell-bent on this, you need to turn south and head into the swamp. I don't know if you'll find much of a trail once you get there, but that's the place you should look." He paused and looked away. "I don't never go in there. Nobody does."

"Thanks," Bones said.

"You see them two pines that are leaning together?" Jack pointed deeper into the woods. "You want to walk right under them and that'll put you on the game trail that takes you where you need to go."

"Got it." The kid didn't seem the handshaking type, so Bones made a curt nod and turned the group south. He kept his eyes on the ground, watching for signs to confirm they'd been steered in the right direction.

"You think he knows what he's talking about?" Slater asked as soon as they were out of earshot.

"He seems to know his stuff. Worse case, we retrace our steps and find the trail again." He glanced back over his shoulder. Jack was gone. "He can move in the woods,

I'll give him that much."

"There's the two pine trees. The game trail should be right through there." Dave quickened his pace and moved ahead of Bones and Slater just as they passed beneath the pine arch.

Bones smirked at the cameraman and returned his eyes to the path in front of him. Something wasn't right.

"Stop!" He dove forward and grabbed Dave by the belt just as the ground disappeared between the cameraman's feet.

Dave cried out in alarm, his arms pinwheeling as he slid forward, his fall not fully arrested by Bones' strong grasp.

Slater sprang to Bones' side and grabbed hold of one of Dave's flapping arms. "Hold still," she hissed. Together, she and Bones pulled the young man out of the dark hole that gaped beneath him. Once he was free, he lay back, breathing hard.

What... was... that?" he gasped.

"A Burmese tiger pit," Bones said, staring down at the dark hole that had been only partially uncovered by Dave's fall. "You dig a hole, put sharpened stakes at the bottom, and cover it with twigs, leaves, and dirt. Someone comes along and falls right in." He knelt for a closer look. "This one is deep and there are no stakes at the bottom, just a lot of muck since we're so close to the swamp. It's not a killing pit."

"So what is it for?" Carly asked.

"Trapping. Bones and Slater exchanged a dark look.

"So, was the kid trying to trap us?" she asked.

"I don't know. How about I ask him?" Bones made to rise but Slater put a hand on his arm.

"Don't bother. He's got a head start and you said he moves well in the woods."

"You don't think I can catch that little assclown?"

Slater smiled. "I'm sure you can, but it'll be a waste of time. He'll just say he didn't know the pit was there."

Bones gritted his teeth and gave a single nod. She wasn't wrong. "It could be that the pit is just there to make outsiders feel unwelcome." He sighed. "I guess we go back to where we left Jack and try to pick up the trail again."

"Um, isn't that a footprint down there?" Carly pointed down the barely-visible game trail. In the middle of a patch of soft earth lay a single, perfect print.

CHAPTER 7

They set to work immediately, their spirits buoyed by the discovery. While Dave filmed, Slater took measurements and photographs, all the while discussing her thoughts regarding the print.

"This print is fourteen inches long," she began. "Not as large as most of the alleged Sasquatch tracks, but certainly large enough to be of interest to us. The toes are elongated, with a pronounced big toe. The depth of the toe prints are not uniform, which is consistent with what we would see with genuine footprints. We don't tend to evenly distribute our weight when we walk, and certain toes dig in deeper than others, just like this print."

She looked up and motioned for Dave to move in closer. "You can also see that the extremely moist earth has preserved portions of the foot's dermal ridges. It requires ideal conditions to preserve these ridges, and the fact that we only see bits of a few here actually adds to the possibility that these prints are genuine. With a forgery, you're likely to see full ridges."

She then set about making a plaster cast of the print. She placed a cardboard ring around the print, leaving extra space at the heel and toe. Next, she took out a small bucket, a package of plaster of paris, and a large bottle of water. She mixed the plaster and water and stirred vigorously, explaining to the camera that plaster of paris begins to set the moment it comes into contact with water, therefore speed is of the essence when casting a print.

After banging her mixing bucket on the ground a few

times to remove the bubbles, she carefully filled the track, starting with the toes and working her way down. She bit her lip as she concentrated on the task, something Bones found very attractive. When she was finished, she explained that the time required for the plaster to set varied depending on the dryness of the ground and air. In this damp environment, it would take a good hour before they could safely remove the plaster, though the curing process would continue for a few days as moisture leached out of the cast.

They took an early lunch while they waited for the cast to set. Despite Bones' warnings that they should remain quiet, the crew was unable to contain their excitement. They chatted about their television show, wondering if further discoveries would merit a two-part episode. Bones remained silent, chewing on beef jerky and washing it down with tepid bottled water. When Slater finally proclaimed the casting ready, she covered it in bubble wrap, slid it inside her pack, and they headed farther down the game trail.

The air grew cooler and the vegetation thicker as they proceeded into the swamp. The soft earth beneath their feet gave a little with each step, lending to the feeling of heaviness all around them. The humid air seemed to weigh them down, and the moss-draped, leaning trees only added to the sensation as they trudged on through a maze of greens, grays, and browns. Little by little, the shafts of sunlight grew fewer and farther between until it felt like twilight lay upon them, though it was barely midday.

As they moved deeper, the musky, earthy aroma of the swamp gradually gave way to a dank smell. The scent grew stronger and Bones stopped, crinkled his nose, and sniffed the air.

"What is that odor?" Slater's face twisted into a 'Tom Cruise just invited me to church' grimace.

The scent grew stronger, pungent. Bones shook his head.

"I don't know. It's not a... get down!"

Bones dove at the television crew, corralling Slater and Carly in his arms and plowing into Dave. The three fell in a heap to the damp earth as a rock the size of Bones' fist smashed into a pine tree where Slater had stood only moments before.

Something flashed through the undergrowth—a shadow of indiscernible shape, moving from left to right.

"Get behind that log." Bones pointed to the remains of a fallen tree a few yards away. Slater and her team scrambled for cover while Bones rolled to his left as another stone flew. It struck the earth with a wet slap like a fist hitting flesh, bounced once, and splashed into the stagnant pool behind him. What living thing could throw that hard? Either Craig Kimbrel had gotten lost on the way to Spring Training or Bones was up against something entirely new. He drew the Recon knife sheathed at his side and crawled in the direction where he'd seen the shadow moments before.

What a time to leave my Glock in the truck.

A third stone came flying out from the dense foliage. This one smashed into a rotten stump a foot from Bones' outstretched hand and stuck there. Bones snatched it free, rolled to his feet, and hurled it with all his might at the spot from which it had come. He heard a slap as it struck something soft, then a deep, chuffing sound that might have been pain or surprise.

Bones let out a roar of defiance and dashed toward the spot, zigzagging here and there to hopefully avoid getting crushed by another flying projectile. Up ahead, the underbrush rustled, the sound fading away as their assailant fled.

Bones chased it a good fifty yards before slowing to a trot and finally stopping. He hadn't seen a thing. Whatever it was that attacked them had simply melted into the forest. It was gone. He supposed he should go back and check on Slater and the others, and then search for any tracks it might have left behind. He sheathed his knife and mopped his brow.

And cried out in surprise when the earth gave way beneath his feet.

CHAPTER 8

Bones had only a moment to realize he was falling before his feet hit something solid. Or somewhat solid, because whatever it was his feet struck held for only a moment before it gave way and he plunged deeper into darkness. He landed hard on his feet, pain shooting along his legs. A splintering crack split the air, and for a moment he thought he'd broken a leg, but he realized it was the sound of breaking wood. He rubbed his leg and the pain soon diminished, leaving behind only a dull ache at the base of his spine.

He looked around, the dim light shining through the hole where he'd fallen illuminating a circle about ten feet wide. He stood on a wooden floor, its boards covered in a thin film of dust. Beneath his feet, a series of cracks spread outward, and he took a step back just in case more open space lay beneath him. He took out his Maglite and shone it around.

"No freaking way."

He was inside a ship, probably sixteenth-century by the looks of the cannon his light fell upon. Sweeping his beam back and forth, he saw several more cannons, some still in their tracks, others lying on the floor. This was the gun deck of a large sailing vessel.

He took a cautious step, and then another. The deck supported his weight. Encouraged, he began to explore. The fact that the deck still hadn't given way beneath all these cannons gave him hope that the structure was sturdy enough to bear the weight of one big Cherokee. He supposed he would find out.

At the far end of the deck, a ladder led up to an open trapdoor. He tested the first rung, found it sturdy, and climbed up. He emerged in another sizeable space. All around, the moldering remains of hammocks dangled from the beams that supported the main deck. Lying on the floor amidst the accumulated silt from centuries of leakage lay the skeletal remains of the crew. Some held pitted swords or rusted knives, while others lay curled in fetal balls.

The ceiling up above was blackened with soot. Apparently the crew had made their homes here after being run aground, but how in the hell had a ship gotten this far inland?

"Must have been one hell of a storm," he mumbled.

He shone his beam down to the far end of the deck, where a door hung haphazardly on broken hinges. That would be the officers' quarters. He picked his way across the deck, reluctant to tread on the remains of the deceased. As he skirted the bones of the soldier nearest him, he did a double-take.

The back of the man's skull had been smashed in, leaving a baseball-sized hole.

"What in the..." He knelt for a closer look. The back of the skull had been caved in. Fragments of bone lay inside the hollow of the cranium. Whatever had delivered the fatal blow had compressed the skull. The victim had died lying face-down, and as the soft tissue decayed, the fragments of bone had simply fallen into the hollow space once occupied by the brain.

"Sorry, bro," he said. "That's a nasty way to die."

He stood and resumed his careful trek. It quickly became apparent that every member of the crew had died in the same way—their skulls crushed by a blunt object. He shivered, the fresh memory of flying stones strong in his mind. This ship had been here for a good four hundred years. Could there possibly be a connection? He didn't want to believe it, but he knew better than to dismiss the improbable.

"Bones!" Slater's voice called out from somewhere above. "Where are you?"

"I'm down here!" he called. "But don't come any closer. The ground's not stable."

He moved toward the hole through which he'd initially tumbled, but before he could get there, a pair of hiking boots slid through the opening, followed by trim, deeply tanned legs. Slater!

"Hold on a second. There's a hole right below your feet and you'll fall through if you're not careful. Believe me, I know from experience." He hurried over to her, stumbling over the rib cage of a dead sailor. He reached up, grabbed Slater by the waist, and guided her down to the deck.

Her eyes grew wide as she took in their surroundings. "Where are we?" she marveled.

"Inside an old sailing ship. I'm not sure what kind, exactly."

Slater rounded on him, hands on hips. "A sailing ship? Underground? Are you winding me up?"

"Nope. Check it out." He swept his light across the deck and over the remains of the crew.

"Wow!" Slater gaped, her voice soft and her eyes wide. "How do you think it got here?"

"The only theory I can come up with is one hell of a hurricane carried them inland and they got stuck here when the water receded. It looks like they decided to live inside the ship. You can see they had fires in here." He pointed to the blackened beams up above. "Over time, it sank down into the swamp and the mud preserved it."

"This is amazing. I don't care if it has nothing to do with the skunk ape, it's still going to make for an amazing story." She turned and barked out a sharp command. "Dave! Carly! Get down here. I want this all on video."

"Be careful," Bones called. "Let me help…"

With a hollow crack, the main deck above them gave way again and Dave came crashing down on top of them. Bones managed to wrap his arms around the young cameraman and partially slow his fall, but Dave still landed hard on his backside. Bones froze, wondering if the force of the fall would cause the deck to give way again. This time, it held.

Carly followed, more carefully than her colleague. Bones sat her down lightly on her feet, and she stared in wide-eyed amazement at the macabre scene.

"This is like a haunted house," she breathed.

"More like the Pirates of the Caribbean ride," Dave said, climbing to his feet. "You know, the part where they all turn into skeletons?"

"How about we focus on doing our jobs?" Slater rode over her crew's conversation. "You can talk about amusement parks later."

"Sorry." Dave's gaze dropped to the floor, but he brightened almost immediately. "This is going to be some of the best footage we've ever gotten." He made a slow circuit of the deck, recording every inch of the bizarre scene. He lingered over the fire pit in the center.

The crew had piled a thick layer of sand on the deck to prevent the wood from catching fire. Chunks of bone poked out of the silt and ash. When Slater was satisfied that they had enough footage, they moved on to the officers' quarters.

Inside, they found more skeletal remains, all with smashed skulls.

"It's strange," Slater observed, "that some are lying curled up in a ball. Do you think they just curled up and waited to be killed?"

"Possibly," Bones said, "if they were frightened enough. We don't know how long they holed up here. It's possible some of the crew were already dead from malnutrition or disease, and whoever did this to them bashed their heads in just to make sure."

"Scary stuff." Slater led her crew around the cabin, commenting on the few artifacts she found lying about. The officers' personal effects were few, but among them were knives, rings, Spanish coins, and crumbling bibles. "It's clearly a Spanish galleon. And the fact that things like this remain," she held up a fat gold coin, "proves that we are the first to find it. If its presence had been discovered before, it's almost a guaranteed the valuables would be long gone."

They ascended to the captain's cabin, which lay just above the officer's quarters. The door was wedged closed, and Bones finally resorted to main force to smash open the top half of the decaying wood.

"Looks like somebody blocked themselves in," he said, looking down at the footlocker and small chest that pushed up against the base of the door. But that wasn't the only thing that had held the door fast. Here, the intrusion of years of silt was clearly evident, as a thick layer of dried black muck caked the floor. Bones climbed over the remaining portion of the door and then helped the others in.

The captain lay on his bed, his empty eye sockets gazing up at the ceiling. Dave moved in with the camera while Slater resumed her hosting duties.

"At first glance it looks like the captain also had his skull smashed." She pointed his shattered left temple. "But that isn't the case. If you look at the other side of his head, you'll see a smaller hole. And then there's this." She pointed an object half-buried in the muck. "It's a pistol, lying roughly where it would have fallen from limp, dead fingers."

"So he barred himself inside and took his own life." Dave said the words slowly as if trying to convince himself of their veracity.

"Whatever was outside that door was more terrible than the prospect of suicide." Slater turned to Bones. "Can you tell us anything about the gun?"

"It's a matchlock." Bones knelt beside the weapon but left it untouched. "The matchcord, which was just a burning wick, went here," he pointed to the hammer. "It came down and hit the flash pan which ignited the gunpowder. That's about all I can tell you."

"Does the type of gun give us any clue as to the age of the wreck?"

Bones nodded. "By the early 1600s, matchlocks were out and flintlocks were in, so this is probably sixteenth century."

An inspection of the captain's truck revealed little of interest, but the small chest was filled with coins, many of them silver and gold. Bones resisted the urge to pocket a few. Maybe when the camera was no longer rolling.

"Where to next?" Slater asked.

"All the way to the bottom," Bones said.

"What do you expect to find down there?"

He grinned. "The cargo hold."

CHAPTER 9

Of all the various parts of the galleon, the cargo hold had suffered the most from the intrusion of soil and water. Toward the bow of the ship, where the hull had been split when the ship ran aground, the dark mud lay knee deep, descending to a depth of several inches toward the stern. But it did little to cover the crates that lay all around, scattered and broken by the wreck so many centuries ago.

Carly clapped her hands and Dave let out a whoop of triumph as the beam of Bones' light glinted off blocks of gold and silver bullion and scattered gold chains. Here and there, jewels sparkled like stars in the dark mire. Trying but failing to suppress a grin, Slater discussed the find at length for the benefit of the camera.

"Why so many gold chains?" Dave asked.

Bones knew the answer to this one. "Tax evasion. The Spanish crown placed a tariff on precious metals, but jewelry was exempt. Europeans didn't do much in the way of fine craftsmanship in the New World, but they could make rough chains and rings like what you see here, and that was good enough to get around the law."

"Why not make it all into jewelry?" Carly asked.

"I guess it's one of those things you can only take so far. The crown would look past a certain amount of circumvention as long as it made its share from the transportation of New World treasure, but if it got out of hand, they'd have eliminated the exemption. Nobody wanted to be the one that killed the goose that laid the golden egg."

"Speaking of eggs," Slater said. "Have you seen anything like this before?" She pointed to a small crate filled with dirt, straw, and mud-encrusted egg-shaped objects caked in mud.

"I've never seen one up close, but I've read about them." He knelt beside the crate, took out his recon knife, and scraped away the mud that encased one of the strange objects. "These are bezoars."

"You're kidding," Dave and Carly said in unison.

"What are bezoars?" Slater asked.

"Somebody hasn't read Harry Potter," Dave said.

"A bezoar is a sort of stone formed from material found in the digestive tracts of two-stomached animals. Given that this is a Spanish ship, we're probably looking at stones from a llama or alpaca since those were found in the major Spanish colonies. And, just like in Harry Potter, people believed a bezoar could absorb poison. Somebody rich enough to buy one would dip it in his cup of wine before drinking it, just in case his enemies had tried to poison his cup."

"I take it they were pretty valuable?" Slater asked.

"Very, and not just because of their supposed properties. Being able to afford one was a status symbol. People would have them carved, mounted in a gold setting, and would wear them as jewelry."

"Did they work?" Dave asked. "I mean, do they really absorb poison?"

Bones chuckled. "Tell you what. When we get back to town, we'll put rat poison in a beer, drop one of these in, and you can drink it. Sound good?'"

Dave laughed. "I'll pass." With that pronouncement,

he cut the camera. "Does this mean we get, I don't know, salvage rights or whatever?"

They all looked at Bones, the only treasure hunter in the group.

"If we were three leagues out in the gulf waters or three miles off the Atlantic coast, things would be a lot simpler. On land it's a little more complicated."

"But, finders keepers, right?" Carly asked.

"Not necessarily. A lot depends on who owns the property. If we're still inside the state park, Florida treasure trove law says that whatever we find belongs to the state."

"That's not fair," Dave said.

"That's just the way it is. The good news is, the common practice here is for the government to keep everything of historical value and give the finder seventy-five percent of the intrinsic value of the find."

"What if we're on private property?" Carly asked.

"It probably goes to the owner. There would definitely be a legal battle."

"And since we're doing this under the auspices of the television show, there are other ownership angles to consider," Slater said. "This could be a mess."

"So, maybe we're rich and maybe we're not," Dave said. "It's Schrödinger's treasure."

"I'm sure this will sort itself out eventually," Slater said. "But for now, I say we cover up the holes where you two klutzes fell through, and get back to the job at hand."

Bones nodded. "I want to track down whatever it was that attacked us."

"You think it was a 'what' and not a 'who'?" Carly asked.

Bones merely nodded.

They made their way back up to the crew deck and Bones helped Slater and then Carly climb out. Both were light and agile so it required little effort. Getting himself and Dave out would take a little more creativity.

"Let's gather all the boards and crates we can. We'll pile them up and climb out that way. If that doesn't work, we'll have to dig up enough dirt to make a mound that we can get up on, and hope it isn't so heavy that it causes the floor beneath it to collapse."

He waited for Dave to reply, but no response was forthcoming. The young cameraman knelt by the old fire pit, poking at the bones that lay there. "Take a look at this." He held up a thick leg bone—a femur if Bones didn't miss his guess. "It's got cuts all over it—signs that the meat was butchered. We've seen this before on the show. Cannibalism."

Frowning, Bones took the femur from Dave and gave it a close look. "Maybe not cannibalism."

"But the cuts..."

"You're not wrong about the cuts," he said. "But I don't think this is human. At least not human as we know it."

CHAPTER 10

"**Let me get** this straight," Slater said. "You think this is a bone from a primitive form of hominid?" Slater asked. She turned it over in her hands, scrutinizing every inch of its length. Nearby, Dave kept the camera rolling.

"That's what it looks like to me. Of course, it's the actual bone, not just a fossil, which means it's not very old."

"About as old as the ship?" Dave offered.

Slater nodded. "Mister Gambles did mention the theory that the skunk ape is, in fact, a form of human ancestor. Between the footprint and this bone, we should be able to put that theory to the test." She looked directly into the camera, her jaw set and her gaze hard. "We now have to consider the possibility that the stranded crew sealed their own fate by killing and eating one of the local population of whatever hominid the skunk ape might be."

Quieted by dark thoughts, the group retraced its steps and waited while Bones searched around until he picked up the trail of the fleeing attacker. He found no clean prints, but more than enough sign to guide them in the proper direction. As they followed the tracks, the dank swamp began to dry up, and eventually gave way to forest.

It was early afternoon when Bones spotted something in the distance. "Somebody lives here."

Up ahead, in a clearing, stood an old mobile home. A sagging, makeshift covered porch sheltered the front door. A rusted out 1968 Camaro stood on blocks amidst a patch of tall weeds. Behind the trailer, a decrepit outbuilding hugged the tree line where the forest resumed. To the south, a rutted dirt road wended its way into the dense foliage and vanished from sight.

"I wonder who lives here," Slater whispered.

"I don't know, but it's a shame they didn't restore that Camaro. What a waste." Bones moved a few steps forward, still scanning the ground. "The tracks end here. Whatever we're chasing, it must have skirted the clearing."

"We'll see if anyone's home," Slater said. "They might have seen something."

"Does anyone have dueling banjos playing in their head right now, or is it just me?" Dave whispered.

Carly giggled. "I'll bet you'd be good at squealing like a pig."

Dave raised his middle finger and kept the camera rolling.

Tension cramped Bones' shoulders as they strode across the intervening space between the tree line and the old mobile home. His eyes flitted about, keeping alert for danger. Slater noticed.

"What's wrong?" she asked. "It's just a house."

"I've got a feeling that, any second now, some dude in a John Deere hat is going to jump out of the woods with a shotgun and start blazing away."

Slater chuckled but Dave missed a step and Carly's eyes grew wide.

"I was kidding about the banjos. Do you really think it's dangerous?" Dave asked.

"Probably not. It's just that redneckish places like this put me on edge."

The sagging steps up to the front porch creaked under Bones' weight, but they supported him. Just as he reached the porch, Slater grabbed him by the arm.

"Let me. I don't look as intimidating as you." She winked and slipped past Bones, who backtracked down the steps and moved to stand beside Dave.

Slater knocked, a dull sound in the quiet clearing

No answer.

She knocked again.

"I don't think anyone's home." A note of hopefulness rang in Dave's voice. "Let's just keep following the trail."

"Third time's a charm." Slater raised her fist to knock again, but the door flew open and an angry face poked out.

"This is private property. What are you doing here?" The speaker was a white-haired woman no more than five feet tall. Sharp blue eyes gleamed in the midst of a craggy, sun-weathered face.

Slater introduced herself and explained that they were a television crew investigating local legends. If she thought her fringe Hollywood credentials would earn her any points with this woman she was mistaken.

"I don't know no legends. You need to get on out of here before I call the sheriff."

"I done called him, Granny." A familiar figure appeared in the doorway. "He'll be here any second." Jack froze when his eyes fell on Slater. "What are *you* doing here?"

"You know these people, Jack?" The old lady rounded on her grandson, eyes flashing.

"He tried to kill us," Bones said.

"I didn't!" Jack took a step back, but his grandmother

snatched him up by the hair and hauled him out on the porch with surprising strength.

"Were you messing around with that rifle again? I done told you, it's for hunting and nothing else. If you can't be responsible I'm going to take it back from you." She glanced at Bones. "I'm surprised the big fellow didn't take it away from you and whoop your butt with it."

Bones chuckled. He decided he liked this lady.

"Actually, he directed us right into a tiger trap," Slater said.

Jack held up his hands. "I didn't know that pit was there. Ow!"

His grandmother gave his hair a twist and then let him go. "You knew. Now go fetch me a switch." As Jack trudged down the steps and toward the woods, head hung low, she folded her arms and addressed the group. "I hope none of you have any objection to some old-fashioned discipline. The boy ain't got no mama and someone's got to teach him to mind."

"I've lost count of how many times I've been switched in my life," Bones said. "Even now I think my grandfather would whip me if I stepped out of line."

"If you don't mind my asking," Slater began, "have you seen anything unusual here?"

"Unusual?"

"Something attacked us in the woods. We followed its trail which led us here. I'm just wondering if you saw who or what did it."

The old woman shook her head. "Just me and Jack here."

"The pit we fell into, what's it for?" Slater asked.

The sound of a car approaching drew their attention

and they turned to see a police cruiser rolling slowly up the driveway.

"You'll have to ask him." That ended the conversation as she stepped back inside and closed the door.

The car rolled to a stop and Deputy Logan stepped out and closed the door behind him. He pocketed his sunglasses and took a seat on the hood of his car.

"You mind telling me what you're doing here?"

"We're doing an investigation," Slater said, coming down off the steps. "Something attacked us in the park. We followed its tracks which led here."

"What do you mean by attacked?" Logan' kept his tone level but something in his eyes suggested alarm, even fear.

"Something was chunking rocks the size of my fist at us," Bones said. "Any one of them could have killed us."

"Don't you mean 'someone'? There's not an animal around here that can throw a rock, unless the gators have figured out how to slap them with their tails."

Slater cocked her head. "Isn't there?"

"What's that supposed to mean?" Logan snapped.

"Deputy," Bones began, "there's not a man alive who could throw a rock that big with the velocity those things were flying at our heads."

"We also found footprints." Dave piped up.

Slater turned a hard eye on her cameraman, whose face reddened.

"I'm going to have to ask you to turn over anything you collected," Logan said. "Video, photographs, cameras, cell phones and especially any castings you made of tracks."

"On whose authority?" Bones resisted the urge to get in the deputy's face.

"The county sheriff's department, that's who." Logan rested his hand on his sidearm. "Don't make me arrest you."

Slater moved between Bones and the deputy. "First of all, you and I both know the law. You don't have probable cause to confiscate our property. Second, everything is already uploaded to the cloud—photos, video, audio, all of it. Taking our belongings would be a waste of your time and ours, and it would make unwanted publicity for your department."

Logan' jaw worked as he stared past Slater at Bones.

"We might as well tell them, Pa." Jack's voice broke the tension as the young man slunk out of the woods, trailing a long, thin stick behind him.

"He's your kid?" Bones asked.

Logan nodded.

"Tell us what?" Slater asked.

"Nothing." Logan said.

"Just go on and tell them." Jack's grandmother called out the front window. "You knew it couldn't last forever."

Logan' shoulders sagged. "I suppose you're going to find out sooner or later. Turn your camera on and let's get this over with." He flashed a rueful grin at Slater, who stared at him with a bemused expression. "You ain't figured it out yet?"

Slater shook her head.

"The skunk ape is just a myth. We've been faking it."

CHAPTER 11

Slater appeared poleaxed. After a few seconds of stunned silence, she found her voice.

"Who is *we*?"

"Me and my boy." Logan pointed at Jack. "But before we go any further I have to ask that you don't show my face or give my name. Don't show my house, either. I want that in writing."

Slater sighed. "Fair enough. I'll even change your voice. Hold on a minute." She dug a few papers out of her backpack and she and Logan took a few minutes to complete them. When all was ready, Logan led them to the outbuilding behind the trailer.

"This is where we keep our stuff." He unlocked a metal gun cabinet and took out a pair of false feet. They were made of some sort of rubber, and were intricately detailed. All the lines and creases one would expect to see in an actual foot were carefully rendered. The big toe was angled downward so it would bite deeper into the earth than would the other toes. Velcro straps extended from the rubber on either side. Presumably the wearer could strap them to whatever shoes he had on.

Bones took one and looked it over. It was about the size of the other prints they'd seen. It certainly could have been the source.

"What about weight distribution?" Slater asked. "If someone with an average sized foot wears this, the weight will be too close to the center."

"It's got a metal frame inside. It distributes the weight but still has a little flexibility."

"Where'd you get it?" Slater asked.

"I had it made, but that's all I'll say. I don't want to bring anyone else into this"

Slater nodded. "But why go to all this trouble? What did you hope to gain?"

Logan smiled sheepishly. "I could tell you it was about publicity for the town, or to keep a favorite legend alive, but it wouldn't be true. The fact is, I did it because I thought it was funny. It started out as a way of messing with campers. Rattle the bushes, leave a couple of tracks, and get out of there." He chuckled. "I got bored with it, but then I started hearing about a fellow named Gambles who was taking the skunk ape thing way too seriously, so I decided to mess with him too."

"We met him," Slater said. "He'll be disappointed when he hears."

"Don't bet on it. He's one of them true believers. If he doesn't want to hear it, it'll just bounce right off of him." Logan looked down and scuffed the dirt with his booted toe. "Anyway, I started feeling bad about that, but then Jack got curious, so I let him do it sometimes."

"What about the strong smell?" Carly chimed in.

"Bobcat urine, fox urine, whatever the store's got in stock."

"You can buy that stuff?" Dave asked.

"People use it to keep pests away," Bones said. He handed the false foot to Slater, turned, and took a few steps back to the shed door where he leaned against the frame and gazed out at the late afternoon sun. Jack was approaching, walking gingerly and grimacing. Apparently his grandmother had put the switch to use. The sight of the boy sparked something in his mind.

"So, which one of you attacked us today?"

"It must have been the boy." Logan spat on the ground. "I'm sorry about that. I'm sure he wasn't trying to hurt you; he just has bad aim with that sling of his."

"A slingshot couldn't throw a stone as large as the ones that were hurled at us, much less achieve the velocity," Slater said. "Those things were really flying. It's no exaggeration to say we could have been killed."

"Not a slingshot. A sling. You know, like David and Goliath. They're easy to make."

"I don't see how Jack could have done it," Bone said, turning back to face Logan. "This place is a long way from where we ran into him. How could he have come here, gotten what he needed, and then gotten back in time to attack us?"

"It's not a long way if you know where you're going." Jack had arrived at the shed. "I knew I'd left some prints in the swamp, so I sent you that way and then ran home to get my stuff. I figured I'd track you down and mess with you a little. I flung a few rocks at you and then took the long way home. You were following my trail which is why it took you so long."

"We *did* take a lunch break while you made the casting of the footprint," Bones said to Slater.

"But still..." Slater began.

Bones shook his head. "It doesn't matter. We've solved the mystery. I'm sorry it's not what you hoped it would be but at least you have your answer."

"I'll give you all a ride back to your car," Logan said.

"That won't be necessary." Slater bit off each word. "We can find our way back."

"Please. I've done you wrong. At least let me do this

one little thing for you." He grinned at Bones. "I also won't make an issue of the incident that happened at the river." He waited for Bones to fill the silence, but Bones knew that trick and held his tongue. "Two boys said a great big Indian jumped them and stole their truck keys. Had to pay a locksmith to cut a new set."

"It serves them right," Carly said.

Logan laughed. "I'm sure it does. Them two are no good. I've been dealing with them for years. Now, how about that ride?"

CHAPTER 12

The alarm on his phone vibrated. Bones rolled out of bed and shut it off. Midnight. Time to move.

While the Keurig in his hotel room brewed a cup of strong coffee, he bathed his face in cold water and then trickled a little down the back of his neck for good measure. He'd reluctantly declined Slater's invitation to dinner in favor of an early bedtime, knowing he'd be up in the middle of the night. When his coffee was ready, he grabbed it along with his keys, strapped on his Recon knife, pocketed his MagLite, and headed out the door.

The soupy Florida air enveloped him in its damp arms the moment he stepped out the door. No matter how long he lived, he doubted he'd ever grow accustomed to the humidity. He spared one longing thought for the lumpy mattress and blasting air conditioning in his room, and then closed the door behind him.

"I knew you didn't buy his story," said a soft voice.

Bones grinned. "I wondered why you gave up so easily." He turned to see Slater sitting on the floor, back against the door of her room. Smiling, she cracked open a can of energy drink.

"I didn't want to pound this baby until I was sure you were coming out."

"Drink it slow. Those things will mess you up." Bones winced at the sound of his words. Caution was Maddock's thing, not his.

"Understood. Help me up?" She reached out a hand and Bones hauled her to her feet. "So, what's the plan?"

"Here, I'll show you." He took out his phone and called up the map he'd studied earlier. "Logan' house is here, near the bend in the Myakka River. This area here is pure swamp—it's a no-man's land all the way to the spot where I estimate the sunken galleon sits, and well beyond. I think it's worth checking out. We'll park down the road from Logan' house and try and find the trail."

Forty minutes later, Bones pulled his truck off to the side of the rutted dirt road that led to Logan' home. He pulled it into the woods out of sight of the main road and cut the engine.

"Do you want to wait here while I see if I can pick up the trail?" he asked Slater.

"Not a chance. You'll go on without me and I'll be left sitting here looking like an idiot." She reached into her backpack and took out a small handheld video recorder.

"No cameras," Bones said.

"What are you talking about?"

"This isn't for the show. This is about satisfying my own curiosity." He saw the hard look in her eyes. "If you bring a camera, I'll just slip off into the woods and leave you wandering til morning."

Slater looked like she might take that as a challenge, but then her shoulders sagged and she returned the camera to its bag. "You're an ass, you know that?"

"I know. My sister reminds me every chance she gets."

Slater cocked her head. "You have a sister? What's she like?"

"Pretty like you; abrasive personality like me." While

Slater chewed on that, he reached into the glove box and took out his Glock. He checked the magazine and then slipped the holster onto his belt.

"You're not thinking about shooting Logan, are you?"

"I'm not thinking of shooting anybody. I just want to have the option in case we're forced to defend ourselves. Come on. We're wasting time."

Using only the moonlight to illuminate his path, he led the way into the woods. A few minutes later, the mobile home loomed in the distance. A single light glowed from somewhere inside, but otherwise all was dark and quiet.

"Do you need my flashlight?" Slater whispered.

"I've got it covered." He took out his MagLite, into which he'd slipped a red lens, and turned it on. "White light would draw too much attention and would screw up my night vision. This way we're unlikely to be spotted."

"You're smarter than you look."

"And you're not," he replied with a wink.

"Point for your side."

Bones carefully searched the area behind the outbuilding where Logan had shown them the false feet earlier that day. Finally, he came across a partial print, and then another.

"We've got a trail," he whispered.

"That took a long time. Think we'll be back in time for breakfast?"

"I always tell a lady to plan on being out all night. This time is no different." He winked, though he was sure she couldn't see it in the dark. "If we're lucky, the tracks follow that trail up ahead." He pointed to a game trail that wound off into the forest.

They hurried along, and Bones was encouraged to find enough tracks and sign to keep them moving at a steady clip. Whatever had passed this way, it had been in a hurry. Here and there he picked up shoe prints the size of a youth or a small man. Jack had been this way.

The path curved around to the southeast, bending back toward the swamp. The air grew dank and the ground sloppy.

"Do you think we're headed back toward the old ship?" Slater asked.

Bones shook his head. "Wrong direction. I think..." He froze. A powerful stench wafted through the night air. "Get down." He put his hand on Slater's shoulder and forced her down into a crouch.

"Do you see something?"

"Not yet. I caught a whiff of something so I'm playing it safe. I don't want any big rocks flying at our heads." He waited, looking and listening, but nothing seemed to be about. "I guess we follow our noses." He turned out his MagLite, drew his Glock, and began to move forward.

"Don't use your gun on them," Slater pleaded.

"Not unless it's in defense of our lives. I generally don't relish killing. There have been a few people I didn't mind taking out, but they all deserved it."

"If you say so."

The trail soon disappeared, giving way to soggy earth that squelched with each step, threatening to suck the boots off of their feet. Slater let out a small gasp of surprise as she suddenly found herself ankle-deep in muck.

"So gross." She grimaced as she slowly worked her foot out of the mire. "We won't be able to go much farther, I don't think."

"Don't be so sure. There are stepping stones up ahead." The faint slivers of moonlight cast a thin, silver glow on a line of flat stones in the midst of the swamp.

"Where do you think it goes?" Slater asked.

Bones took a deep breath. "Only one way to find out."

CHAPTER 13

Bones took the steps with painstaking care, trying hard to make no sound as he crept forward. The stepping stones led them on a curving path through the black water, bending around ancient oak and cypress and beneath gray curtains of Spanish moss, until the way suddenly opened up and Bones froze.

Before them lay an island in the middle of the swamp. Dotted with huge oak trees, their overlapping branches forming a roof-like canopy, the place was well hidden, even from above. The odor he now associated with the skunk ape hung heavy in the air.

"Should we go closer?" Slater whispered.

"Let's wait a minute." He turned out his light and allowed his eyes to fully adjust to the darkness.

The largest oak at the center of the island was hollowed out at the base, cave-like. As he watched, he saw something move there. Slater grabbed his wrist and squeezed. She saw it too.

Something emerged from the darkness out into the moonlight. Its shape was vaguely human, with cords of muscles knotting its broad shoulders, short neck, and powerful arms and legs. A thatch of thick hair hung down to its shoulders, but otherwise it had little more body hair than an adult *homo sapiens*. Its brow jutted out in a prominent ridge, shading eyes that were mere pools of black in the dim light.

"Oh my God." Slater's faint voice scarcely reached his ear. "It really is a primitive human. But what kind is it? *Neanderthal? Cro Magnon*? Something else?"

"I don't know. It's not exactly my area of expertise."

Slater continued to grip his wrist. "But humans didn't come to the Americas until late in history. They were Paleo-Indians, not primitive hominids."

"I guess that theory needs revising. Trust me, it's far from the strangest thing I've ever learned."

Bones continued to gaze at the creature, mesmerized by its presence, by its very reality. The thing walked hunched over, sometimes scurrying on all fours, other times loping along on two legs as it moved back and forth along the waterline. Finally it picked up a long, pointed stick, and returned to the edge of the water. A faint sliver of silver light shone on its face, and Bones finally got a good look at it.

"I think it's young. No facial hair, not a lot of body hair either."

It squatted there, its prominent jaw working as it gazed intently at the water. Slowly it raised the sharpened stick.

"What's it doing?" Slater asked.

In a flash, it brought the stick down, and drew it back to reveal a skewered fish flopping at the end.

"Fishing." Bones grinned and turned toward Slater. "What are you doing?"

Slater held her phone up, recording video of the scene.

"I have to." She snatched the phone in close to her body and took a step back. "This is too incredible to just ignore. I can't pretend... whoa!" She stepped backward into the water, her arms flailing as she struggled to regain her balance, and her phone went flying. Bones managed to catch her before she fell. "My phone!" she cried.

Before Bones could tell her to forget the phone, the creature on the island let out a low, guttural cry.

"It heard you. Look out!" They ducked. A moment later, one of the now-familiar stones flew through the air and smacked into a cypress tree.

"Sorry," Slater whispered.

"Let's get out of here. Stay low."

Slater turned but before she could take a step another stone splashed into the water inches from her feet.

Bones drew his Glock. He didn't want to do this, but he was not going to let them die here. He took aim as the creature reached back to throw again. If it forced his hand...

"Bones, wait!" Slater grabbed the barrel of the Glock and tried to force it down. "Look over there." She nodded toward the hollowed-out tree.

Another creature emerged, this one clearly an older female. She held an infant to her breast. She grunted something that must have been language, because the young male dropped the stones he was holding and scurried away.

A few moments later, another creature appeared, this one an older male. He was huge—much broader and more muscular than the young male. The footprints they had found must have been his.

He reached the female's side and put an arm around her. The intimacy...the humanness of the moment took Bones' breath away. He holstered his pistol and rose to his feet. The two creatures met his gaze, and he thought he saw sadness and resignation there.

"Do you think there are any more?" Slater whispered.

"I don't see any." Bones was surprised to hear a catch in his voice. Was this the last, tiny remnant, of a primitive people who'd called this swamp home?

"Let's just leave them alone." Slater said. She took his hand, and they turned and retraced their steps out of the swamp.

CHAPTER 14

Logan was seated on the tailgate of Bones' truck when they finally reached the dirt road. He was dressed in street clothes and carried no weapon that Bones could see. He and Bones exchanged a long, level stare. Finally, Logan broke the silence.

"How was your hike?"

"A complete waste of time. Nothing but mud out there."

Logan folded his arms and looked up at the sky. "Did you happen to take any pictures or videos of all that nothing?"

Bones shook his head. "Not a thing."

Logan nodded. "How about we quit dancing around each other and just tell the truth?"

"We found them," Slater said, "but we're not going to do anything about it. We don't have any photos or video and we're not going to tell anyone what we saw. As far as we're concerned, the mystery ended when we found out that an unnamed local faked the tracks. That's how the episode of our show is going to play out, anyway."

"Thank you. I mean it." He slid down off the tailgate, walked over, and shook hands with Bones and Slater.

"So, what's the real story?" Bones asked.

"My family's lived on this land for more than a hundred years, and we've known about the skunk apes pretty much the whole time. We've been protecting them, trying to keep people from finding out the real story. It wasn't that hard until Sarasota really started to grow. We still don't get too many folks coming into this neck of the woods, but it happens."

"What's the deal with the fake footprints?" Bones asked. "Seems like that would just draw the kind of attention you don't want."

"We've never made any footprints. Matter of fact, we try to wipe out all we find. That's one of the reasons Jack wanders so far afield. The skunk apes range wide sometimes and we do our best to cover their tracks. The false feet and such, that's stuff I had made in case anyone came snooping around." He flashed them a grin. "If somebody got too close to the truth, I figured I'd tell them me and Jack had faked the whole thing."

"We saw shoeprints leading toward their island," Bones said. "Do you have any interaction with them?"

"Not really. We keep an eye out for them, take them food. Fruit and the like. But we keep our distance."

"Did your family ever consider bringing in someone who could protect them?" Slater asked. "University researchers or a government agency?"

Logan barked a laugh. "Protect? Hell, no. They'd take them away for study. If they really were just a breed of ape that didn't belong here, an exotic species of orangutan or something, that might be one thing, but primitive humans? There's no way the government would pass up a chance to study their genetics and such. They wouldn't leave them out here in the swamp where anyone and anything could get to them."

Bones nodded thoughtfully and scratched his chin. He could think of all kinds of scenarios in which the so-called skunk apes would be in danger if their presence were made known. "You're right. If word got out that they were here, the government would almost have to take them into custody for their own protection. There are too many people who would want to get their hands on them: zoos, private corporations, government groups. Heck, if somebody was violently anti-evolution they might be tempted to come out here and erase the possible evidence."

"I didn't think of any of that," Slater admitted.

"I'm a cynic. I always look on the dark side."

Logan breathed a sigh. "I don't think it's going to matter for much longer. There's only four of them left, and they've been breeding from the same family tree for a couple of generations. The young male had a mate, but a gator got ahold of her. I tried to get to her so I could help her, give her first aid, but they wouldn't let me come close. She bled out." He shook his head slowly, staring at the ground. "I don't know if the baby is male or female. Even if it's a girl and she lives long enough to bear children, it won't matter in the long run. It's almost over for them."

"It's not a breeding population," Slater said. "I understand why you're doing this, but it really seems like a missed opportunity to study a primitive human population."

"We've got years of notes, pictures, and videos our family's taken," Logan said. "We aren't scientists, but somebody will be able to make something of what we've learned when the time comes."

"And when will that be?" Bones asked.

"Whenever the last one dies. Whether it's me, Jack, or Jack's children, the body will go to the Florida Museum of Natural History for study. They can take their DNA and stuff after that. Until then, I say let them be."

Bones and Slater exchanged a long look.

"Agreed," Bones said. "Sorry for trespassing. We just had to know the truth."

"Don't mention it. Sorry you and I got off on the wrong foot."

They bade Logan goodbye and drove back to the hotel in reflective silence. It was a shame, in a way. Mystery solved, and he couldn't tell anyone.

CHAPTER 15

A gentle breeze blew in off the Gulf of Mexico, carrying with it a hint of salt. Bones squeezed a slice of lime into his bottle of Dos Equis and sat back to watch the traffic moving up and down Ocean Boulevard on Siesta Key. A few stray vehicles cruised the street, slowing to check out the girls in shorts and bikini tops walking along the thoroughfare. Bicycles and a few Segways zipped along. From his perch on the blue painted deck of the Siesta Key Oyster bar, it seemed to him a perfect day at the beach.

"I freaking love Siesta Key," Bones said as he winked at a tall redhead who grinned shyly up at him as he passed. "I might move here some day when I'm too old to handle Key West."

"I just wish it wasn't so hot." Dave frowned up at the yellow Landshark umbrella above their table as if offended by the insufficiency of the shade it provided.

"It's Florida. The beach. If you're hot, take off your shirt," Bones said. "That's how it's done down here."

"Please leave your shirt on," Carly said. She took a sip of her margarita and gazed into the distance.

"What's up with you, chick? Didn't get enough sleep last night?"

"I'm just disappointed. When we talked to Gambles, I let myself get excited. I was so sure we were going to find something definite about the skunk ape. Instead we uncovered a hoax."

Bones nodded but didn't comment. He and Slater had decided not to let the others in on their discovery of the previous night.

"Sometimes that's the way things go," Slater said. "In fact, that's usually how it goes. You should know that by now."

"I do," she said. "I just thought this time would be different."

"It'll still make for an interesting episode." Dave absently ran his finger through the beads of condensation on his bottle of Budweiser. "Usually, shows like ours find a few lame-ass clues, exaggerate them, and end the episode without anything definitive. At least we got to the bottom of the mystery. That's something." He closed his eyes and rubbed the bottle against the back of his neck. "Ah! That feels good."

"Seriously, dude, it's not that hot." Bones shook his head and took another drink.

"And there's the pirate ship," Dave said. "Depending on how much footage we use from it, we could make the episode a two-parter. Heck, we could go back and investigate the ship even more. That would make a great episode."

"Speaking of the ship," Slater said, "I've done some checking. The good news is, it's on public land."

Carly's eyes lit up. "So that means the state might give us a cut?"

"The state might give *the show* a cut." Slater let the statement hang in the humid air while she finished off her IPA and motioned for another one. "I made a few calls this morning. Nothing's final, but everyone I spoke to said the producers claim ownership of all discoveries."

They all fell silent, contemplating this bit of news.

"Damn," Dave finally said. "I was this close to being

rich." He held his thumb and forefinger an inch apart.

"I just wanted to get LASIK," Carly said glumly. "I'm sick of these contacts."

Bones decided the time had come to spill the beans.

"I can't make you rich, but I think you'll be able to afford your eye surgery."

Triple frowns bored into him, and he dismissed them with a laugh and a wave. "Check this out." He reached under the table and hefted the backpack he'd worn the previous day. It made a heavy thump when he sat it down, causing the others to flinch. "I don't need to tell you, this is just between us." He unzipped the pack just enough for them to see what lay inside—four gold bars and a handful of Spanish coins.

"You stole that stuff?" Dave's whispered question conveyed a heap of admiration and no criticism.

"I snagged it before we left the cargo hold. The way I see it, it doesn't really belong to anyone. There's still a whole mess of treasure for the government and your producers to fight over, millions upon millions worth, and they'll never know this little bit was gone."

"I have to say I'm surprised and a little uncomfortable," Slater said.

"I get that. I had a misspent youth, and even though I've been straight for a long time, I sometimes stray off the path. You guys can't tell me you couldn't use a little cash."

"I could." Slater spoke deliberately. "But what am I going to do with coins and a gold bar? I can't put them in the bank, or even let anyone know I have them."

"Relax. I've been a treasure hunter since I left the service. I know a guy. Hell, I know several guys."

That broke the tension.

"Cheers!" Dave proclaimed, raising his bottle. They all clinked glasses and laughed.

"Drink up," Bones said. "Next round is on me."

End

AZTLAN- A DANE AND BONES SHORT STORY

By faith we understand that the worlds were set in order at God's command, so that the visible has its origin in the invisible.

Hebrews 11.3

AZTLAN

"**Holy crap, it's** hot out here." Bones Bonebrake mopped his brow and cast a challenging look at the sun high in the cornflower blue sky. "And don't give me that 'It's a dry heat' stuff. Hot is hot."

"No argument here." Dane Maddock plucked at the neck of his sodden shirt. It wouldn't stay damp for long in this dry climate. He hunkered down on the tiny rock ledge where they'd stopped to take a breather, took a bottle of water from his pack, and took a long drink. He gazed out at the parched red landscape of southern Utah. Sharp peaks and low hills dotted the horizon, all shades of the same reddish-brown as the mountainside on which they perched. It had been a long time since he'd ventured into this part of the country, and he realized he'd missed the open skies and sweeping vistas.

"Are we close to the top?"

"Why? Are you ready to wuss out on me?" Bones' heavy breathing belied his bravado.

"Hardly. We both know I'll reach the summit before you do. Why don't you just give it up?"

"Not on your life." The tall, powerfully-built Cherokee squatted down beside Maddock, removed the tie from around his ponytail, and let his long hair blow in the breeze.

The two made an odd pair: Maddock was fair-skinned with blue eyes and short, blond hair. He stood just a shade under six feet tall, but alongside the six and a half foot tall Bones, he looked small.

Bones stood, knuckled his back, and turned to

examine the rock face above them. "Only about fifty meters to go. Shouldn't be too bad."

"Remind me again why we decided to free climb here?" Maddock asked, tucking the water bottle back into his pack and rising to his feet.

"Because no one ever has. Because it's awesome." Bones bared his straight white teeth in a wolfish grin.

"How'd you find out about this place, anyway?"

"My cousin Isaiah." Bones' cousin, Isaiah Horsely, was a professor and archaeologist working the American Southwest. "He found out about it from a local storyteller who says few people even know this place exists."

"I don't wonder," Maddock said. "Considering how much trouble we had just getting here, much less climbing it."

Motec Mountain's height and steep sides made it look less like a mountain and more like a butte that had been stretched out until it touched the sky. Nestled in the heart of Utah's Red Rock region, it was one of the most remote locations Maddock had ever visited in this part of the country.

"He told me some other stuff about it. Legends mostly. Weird stuff but pretty cool."

"Tell me when we get to the top. The longer I stand here, the more I think about the cooler of beer waiting in the car."

"Dude, you can drink beer any time. How often do you get to boldly go where not very many men have gone before?"

Maddock frowned at Bones. "Seriously? We do it all the time."

"And that's why we rule. Now let's get back to climbing."

Upon reaching the summit, Maddock expected to be rewarded with a refreshing breeze and a spectacular view, but he found neither. A fine mist hung over the landscape, slowly swirling in a clockwise pattern and giving the air a tepid quality.

"This is weird." Bones waved his hand in front of his face, the mist curling around his arm. "It's like it wants to grab ahold of you."

"Nothing about this makes sense," Maddock said. "We're in an arid climate. Why doesn't the fog dissipate, or at least burn off? And where is the moisture coming from?"

"The storyteller said there's a lake up here. Want to check it out?"

Maddock gazed at the curtain of mist. It was odd, to be sure, but it didn't seem to be dangerous. Curiosity winning out over caution, he nodded. "Let's see what's up."

The way was smooth, with only a few scattered boulders here and there to impede their way. Though the mist shrouded the landscape in white, it was thin and visibility was more than adequate. Soon they came to the edge of a dark lake.

"Want to go for a swim?" Bones asked.

"I don't know." Maddock felt uneasy as he scanned the surface of the water. He realized in an instant what caused his discomfort. "The water doesn't move at all. Look at it. It's like a sheet of glass."

"Maybe it is." Bones knelt down and touched the

surface. It scarcely made a ripple. "This is jacked-up. It's water, all right, but it's like there's a surface tension holding it in place. I don't know how to describe it."

"I think you describe it just fine," Maddock said, dipping his own finger into the water. "It's warm, too."

"Isn't there a lake in the Middle East where people float really easily?" Bones asked. "You know, like without an inner tube or those water wings you love?"

"The Dead Sea." Maddock ignored his friend's jibe. "But that's because of the high salt content. I don't think that's the deal here."

"If it's all the same to you, I'm not going to taste the water." Bones wiped his hand on his shirt.

"And I think we'll pass on the swimming, too."

They stood and began to walk along the shore. They quickly discovered that the lake was perfectly round, or something close to perfect. As they walked, Maddock's discomfort lessened. Maybe this place was more odd than sinister. None the less, he took a moment to dig into his pack for the dive knife he always carried, and hooked the sheath onto his belt. Bones did the same, and they continued their exploration of the mountaintop.

Maddock estimated they'd reached the side of the lake opposite where they'd begun their circuit when Bones halted in his tracks.

"Look at this."

Maddock followed his friend's line of sight to where a complete skeleton grinned up at them. A tarnished breastplate covered its chest and a tarnished helmet and the rusted remains of a sword lay nearby.

"Spanish," Maddock noted. "Probably an explorer."

"And he climbed all the way up here in his armor?"

Bones said doubtfully. "I'm not buying it."

"It wouldn't be the strangest thing we've seen. Who knows? Maybe there is, or was, another way up."

"I have another idea." Bones folded his arms and turned to face Maddock. "Hear me out on this. This is an alien hot zone." He raised a big hand before Maddock could argue. "Just listen. That could explain the weird water and the mist. And like you said, we've seen enough strange crap that it's not the most far-fetched idea in the world."

"So the aliens abducted the Spaniard and then dumped him here?" Maddock couldn't believe he was indulging his friend's fixation with extraterrestrials, but Bones wasn't wrong. They'd seen and experienced enough strange things that nothing could be discounted.

"Now you're thinking like an honest-to-goodness conspiracy theorist. I knew I'd win you over sooner or later."

"Just trying to follow your train of thought, and believe me, it's a scary ride."

They continued on and made it only twenty or so paces before something on the lake caught Maddock's attention.

"Bones, look at that." Far from the shore, a dark shape loomed in the mist. At their feet, flat round stepping stones formed a bridge.

"Another of the storyteller's details I forgot to mention," Bones said. "There's supposed to be an island in the middle of the lake. And, of course, it's cursed."

"Do you believe in curses?" Maddock asked.

"Other than a woman scorned? Nope." Bones grinned. "Lead the way."

Maddock tested the first stepping stone and found it was solid. He tensed slightly as he put his full weight on it, and relaxed when it held. "I don't know if it'll support your fat butt," he said to Bones, "but I'm good to go."

"Screw you, Maddock."

Maddock almost felt like he was dreaming as he moved through the mist across the motionless lake.

"I bet this is what Heaven is like," Bones said in an uncharacteristically soft voice.

"You'll never find out."

"That's cool. Better parties in hell, anyway."

At the center of the lake, they stepped onto solid stone. It didn't take long to discover that what Bones had believed to be an island was, in fact, a giant stone disc.

"I told you, dude," Bones said. "Aliens."

"Aztecs, more like. See?"

Symbols and other imagery covered the rock beneath their feet. Though he didn't know the meanings of most of them, the patterns and motifs were familiar. "It looks like a giant Aztec Calendar Stone."

"You're right." Bones dropped to one knee to get a closer look. "Doesn't mean aliens didn't help them, though."

"True. Let's keep going."

They moved deeper into the mist and soon the dark form toward which they'd been moving began to take shape. They soon found themselves at the foot of a miniature pyramid. At the top stood a small temple, surmounted by a sculpture of the feathered serpent head of Quetzalcoatl. That sealed it. The site was definitely Aztec.

They climbed the dozen stairs to the top, where, just

inside the temple door, a tight spiral staircase descended into the darkness. They clicked on their mini Maglites and headed down. Time seemed to slow down as they wound deeper into the heart of the mountain, Bones grumbling all the while about the low ceiling and tight quarters.

Finally, they emerged in a large chamber. Maddock halted at the entrance and ran the beam of his light across the floor, looking for potential booby traps, but saw nothing. He took a few cautious steps inside and waited for Bones to join him.

"Interesting," Bones observed, shining his light all around.

The room was round with a low ceiling. Spaced equally were the mouths of seven caves. At the center stood a waist-high pedestal.

"There's an Aztec legend," Bones began, "about a place called Chicomoztoc, or 'The Place of the Seven Caves.' From here, seven tribes, for lack of a better term, came together and settled at Aztlan, the ancestral home of the Aztecs."

"So if this is Chicomoztoc, then you think Aztlan is somewhere around here?" Maddock asked.

"The Aztecs called Aztlan 'The land to the North', and this is well north of Mexico. It was reputed to be an island within a lake." Bones scratched his chin. "And the word itself means 'the place of whiteness.' Think about it: the island within a lake, the white mist, the connection to the caves. I think the island up above us is Aztlan."

Maddock frowned. "But Aztlan is supposed to be the Aztecs' ancestral home. An entire nation couldn't live up there. It's just a single mountaintop."

"You know how legends work. They get passed down from generation-to-generation and it changes a little at a time until it's an entirely different story with only a few recognizable details remaining. Maybe Aztlan was the place the Aztecs emerged from, I don't know, under the earth."

Only a few years earlier Maddock would have scoffed at this, but such a story no longer seemed far-fetched. "Let's check out the caves."

They began by exploring the first cave to their left and quickly discovered that it plunged downward at a steep angle, going on and on with no end in sight. A cursory inspection of the other caves produced similar results.

"This isn't a two-man job," Maddock concluded. "It would take a team, maybe several teams, of researchers to explore this place, depending on how far down the caves go." He turned and shined his light on the pedestal at the center of the main chamber. "Let's check this out."

At first glance, the pedestal was merely a simple cylinder, but closer inspection revealed a detail that had gone unnoticed. At the top, set in the center of the cylinder, was a turquoise disc.

No more than a hand's length across, it was engraved with several symbols. Around the outside ran what looked like a seven-lobed clover. Inside that lay a ring of five suns. Finally, at the center, two figures faced one another. Only a few minor details kept them from being mirror images of one another. The images meant nothing to Maddock, but Bones gasped when his light fell on them.

"Holy crap, Maddock. I know what this is!"

Maddock was not surprised that Bones had some knowledge of Aztec lore. His friend had a keen interest in myths, legends, and ancient prophecies, and the Aztecs were strongly associated with the end of days, and also with aliens, another of Bones' favorite subjects.

"This," he said, hovering a finger over the cloverlike outline, "represent the seven caves. The sunbursts represent the five suns of creation. And they," he pointed at the figures in the center, are Ometecuhtli and his female partner, Omecíhuatl, the highest of the Aztec deities." He looked at Maddock. "This is the Duality Stone."

"What does that mean?"

"I can't say for sure. Only the craziest conspiracy theorist believes it exists." He broke out into a broad grin. "Tell me again what nutbags those guys are."

"You know what they say about a blind squirrel," Maddock said. "But in this case, I tip my cap to you and your eccentric friends."

Bones stood for several moments in silent contemplation. "I think we should tell Isaiah about this place. After all, he's the one who tipped me off about it, and he's got the resources to study it properly.

"Agreed," Maddock said. "This is one heck of a discovery."

The sun was setting over the hills, painting the landscape in shades of orange, by the time they made it back to their vehicle. Both men were utterly spent, yet buoyed by their discovery, their spirits remained high. As they drove along the rutted dirt road back to civilization, Bones spied a small bar. It was a squat, adobe style building of faded brown, nearly the color of the surrounding earth. A faded sign, the paint peeling, proclaimed it the White Bear Pub.

"I don't remember seeing that place on the way here," Bones said. "It's not often that a watering hole escapes my notice."

"It was six in the morning. I hope you weren't keeping an eye out for bars," Maddock said.

Bones nodded thoughtfully. "That must be it. Let's stop for a while."

"We've got beer in the cooler."

"Yeah, but this place has different beer. No reason we can't drink both."

Bones slowed and turned off the main road. He parked alongside the only other vehicle in the dirt lot—an aging sedan of unfamiliar make. As they mounted the single, rickety step up to the building, he glanced back at their rented SUV and frowned.

"I could have sworn we rented a CRV," he said.

"I thought so too." Maddock walked around the back of the vehicle to check the model name. "What the hell is a GAZelle?"

Bones shrugged. "Who knows? Must be a Hyundai or some crap like that. It got us here. That's what matters."

Inside, they found themselves the lone customers inside the dusty bar. Narrow beams of sunlight filtered in through dirty windows, shining on the ceramic tile floor, which was pitted and cracked in places, and setting the dust motes aglow. Maddock and Bones took seats at the bar where the local news was showing on an aging television set.

"Couldn't spring for a flat screen?" Bones asked.

"Don't worry about it."

The bartender, a stout man of late middle years with lightly tanned skin, copious ear hair, and a bald head, greeted them enthusiastically.

"My first customers of the day. I am Alexei. What can I get you?"

Maddock noted a slight Russian accent to the man's speech. Unusual for this part of the country.

"Dos cervezas, por favor." Bones held up two fingers. "Dos Equis if you've got it."

Alexei frowned. "I don't know this beer."

"That's cool. Just give us two of the best beers you've got."

The man smiled and handed them two bottles labeled Tinkoff Golden. Bones tipped him generously and clinked bottles with Maddock. "To discovery."

"Discovery," Maddock agreed. He took a long drink, taking the time to savor the light, tangy flavor. He nodded approvingly and took another drink. "Not bad."

They finished their drinks quickly and Bones called out to the bartender. "Yo, Axel. Another round."

"Alexei," the man corrected though he smiled to show no offense was taken.

"Who's your pick to win the Superbowl this year?" Bones asked, trying to make conversation.

Alexei tilted his head. "You mean the Soccerbowl?"

"What? No, dude. The Superbowl. Football."

"Football and soccer are the same." Alexei picked up a greasy rag and began wiping the counter. "Or do you mean gridiron?" Bones nodded and Alexei grimaced. "Nasty, violent sport. I didn't think they played it anymore."

Bones made a confused face but continued to make small talk with Alexei. Meanwhile, Maddock turned his attention to the television, where the reporter was saying, "Today the American Politburo sent a strongly-worded message to Moscow, warning the Premier that America will not be treated as a lesser member of the Soviet Union."

Maddock almost spilled his beer. Bones had heard too.

"Are we on a hidden camera show?" Bones looked all around.

"I don't understand your jokes," Alexei said, "but I like you all the same."

"You're pretty cool too," Bones said. "Say, who's the president nowadays?"

Alexei cocked his head. "How do you not know that?"

"I can't really talk about it. Let's just say I've been out of circulation for a while."

"No television in prison?" Alexei grinned. "The president is Vladimir Putin."

"I meant the President of the United States."

Alexei laughed. "Now I think I am the one on hidden camera. There has been no president since the war. The American Politburo governs but reports to Moscow, just like all countries in the Soviet Union."

Maddock's head swam and he felt as though his tether to reality was slipping. He took a closer look at their surroundings, truly taking in all the details. Everything was Russian—posters of soccer and hockey teams and framed photographs of Soviet premiers dominated the walls.

Alexei walked away, shaking his head, and Maddock looked at Bones.

"What the hell is going on here?"

Bones stared at him, and then he closed his eyes and let out a groan. "I did it." He buried his face in his hands. "I took the duality stone. It's in my pack. I don't know why I did it. It was like the stone wanted to be taken."

Maddock was surprised at what Bones had done, but that wasn't his primary concern at the moment. "Why should that matter?" he asked.

Bones sighed. "According to legend, the duality stone holds the worlds together." He shook his head. "No, that's not quite right. More like, it tethers the different versions of the world."

"Different versions?"

"You know, like alternate timelines. I know it sounds nuts, but I think it's taken us to a timeline where the Russians won the Cold War."

Maddock looked at the label on his beer and considered what Bones said. Unless they were both experiencing the same hallucination, nothing else made sense. "Maybe we're dreaming," he said lamely.

A sharp pain blossomed in his shoulder. Bones had punched him. "What the hell?"

"Does that feel like a dream?" Bones asked.

"I don't know. Does this?" He returned the favor and Bones winced.

"Okay. We can rule out dreaming."

Alexei, who was polishing the end of the counter, scowled at them. "You fight outside. Not here."

Maddock was about to apologize when his phone

vibrated. He looked at it and his jaw dropped.

"You all right, bro? You're pale as a... well, as a you."

"I just got a text. From Melissa."

Bones looked poleaxed. "That can't be right."

Melissa was Maddock's wife who had died years before.

"If we're in an alternate timeline, maybe she's..." Maddock couldn't say it aloud. Holding his phone in a trembling hand, he read the message aloud.

Hope you can come home soon. We miss you.

"We," he whispered. "Melissa was pregnant when she died. Maybe..."

"Don't do this to yourself, Maddock." Bones said.

Maddock scarcely heard him. He was scrolling through his contact list. He saw familiar names: Bones, Willis Sanders, Pete "Professor" Chapman, and Jimmy Letson.

But he also saw names that hadn't been there before: Hartford Maxwell, their old commander who had been murdered by the Dominion. Franklin Meriwether, a beloved officer who'd died in the Holy Land, and then he gasped.

"Mom and Dad," he breathed. "Bones, look at this! My parents are still alive, and Maxie and Meriwether."

Bones snatched the phone away and scrolled through the list, his brow furrowing deeper as he read. "This is not good."

"What do you mean? Melissa, my parents! Bones, I need to go home."

"Just chill for a second. Listen, we don't belong here. Right now, some alternate Maddock is probably driving home from his job selling insurance, and I'm sure there's another version of Bones who's getting busy with a Russian tennis player. But they're not us and we aren't them."

"How do you know? Maybe the alternate version of us are on a climbing trip in Utah. Maybe we've taken their places."

"It doesn't matter. This isn't our world. Look at this." Bones turned Maddock's phone around so he could see the display. "Yeah, there are some new names here, but you know what? There are some missing too. Matt and Corey aren't here. That means we don't have a crew. There's no Kaylin Maxwell, no Jade, no Tam Broderick. All those mysteries we solved? All we did to fight the Dominion? Never happened. Not here. And there's another important name missing."

They exchanged a level look and Maddock felt his resistance crumbling. He knew precisely who Bones meant. Pain stabbed at his heart. How could he have wanted to stay here, but how could he want to leave?

"Besides, do you really want to live here, under Soviet rule?"

Maddock shook his head. "I suppose not."

Just then, the phone vibrated again. Bones glanced at it and his eyes went wide.

"What is it?"

Bones shook his head. "You're better off not knowing. Trust me."

"Give it to me." Maddock spoke slowly, pronouncing each syllable in a tone that said he would brook no nonsense. Reluctantly, Bones handed it over.

Melissa had texted him again. This time she'd sent a photograph. There she was, her smile and her big brown eyes were just as he remembered. But it was the little boy, a blue-eyed blond who sat on her knee that captivated him. It was his son.

"He looks just like you," Bones said.

Maddock's throat was tight and he only managed a single nod. He felt as if his heart were being torn into a million pieces. It was more than he could take. He took a deep breath and cleared his throat. When he could finally speak, his voice was husky.

"Bones, let's put that stone back where we found it."

The moon hung low on the horizon when they once again emerged from the temple atop Motec Mountain. It shone dully through the mist that still hung over the mountaintop. Between the climbing and the strain of this afternoon's experience, Maddock had nothing left. He crossed the lake and made his way back to the spot where they'd made their ascent only scarcely aware of his surroundings, his mind as foggy as the air that surrounded them.

"I think we should stay here until morning," Bones said. "It's too dark and we're both too tired to climb down."

Maddock nodded and sank to the ground.

"It sucks that we won't know until tomorrow whether we made it home or if we're still stuck in our own version of Red Dawn."

Maddock took out his phone. He scrolled through the contact list and then checked the text messages. The photo and message from Melissa were gone. His list was back to normal, though, and the name at the top brought a smile to his face— Angel.

"It's all right," he said. "We're back."

End

ENJOY THIS PREVIEW OF THE BOOK OF BONES– A BONES BONEBRAKE ADVENTURE

CHAPTER 1

"You've got to be kidding me." Uriah "Bones" Bonebrake stared at the dashboard of his Dodge Ram 1500 pickup truck, watching as the arrow on the speedometer fell while the RPMs red-lined as he stepped down on the gas pedal. Not good. A green road sign loomed up ahead, and he coasted the truck to a stop in front of it.

QUEMADURA, NEW MEXICO 2 MILES

"Almost made it." He consulted his phone and found to his absolute lack of surprise that he had no signal. He'd have to hoof it into town and hope they had a repair place. He could handle minor repairs but, unless he missed his guess, he was looking at something major. He grabbed a bottle of water from the cooler, slung his leather jacket over his shoulder, locked the truck, and headed down the highway.

A stiff breeze took the edge off the hot summer day, but almost immediately, sweat began dripping down his face, only to evaporate in the dry desert air. He dribbled some water on the back of his neck and tried to focus on the landscape.

The golden sun hung high overhead in a cornflower blue sky, shining down on a rolling landscape of juniper, cactus, yucca, and a whole lot of dirt and rock. In the distance, two russet-colored buttes stood out in sharp contrast to the dull brown earth. Because he had nothing else to do, he focused on the hill on the left and tried to estimate its height, then calculated how long it would take him to free-climb the steepest side.

He'd just about completed his estimate when he heard the sound of a vehicle coming up behind him, and turned to see a battered red Honda Accord coming his way. He didn't bother putting out his thumb. Few strangers were comfortable giving a ride to a long-haired, six foot five Native American.

The Accord slowed to a stop alongside him and the driver called out to him. "That your truck back there?"

Bones nodded as he looked the girl up and down. She was Latina with rich caramel skin, full lips, and glossy black hair that hung halfway down her back. She wore a pink midriff tank top, tight-fitting blue jeans, and big sunglasses.

"Yep. That's me."

"Out of gas? In this part of the country you've got to fill up every chance you get. Service stations are few and far between."

"I wish. It's something mechanical for sure."

"Sorry to hear that. Hop in and I'll give you a ride."

Bones heard the passenger door unlock, and he slipped inside. The air conditioning was running at full blast but produced little in the way of cool air. It was in dire need of juicing up, but from the looks of the girl's battered vehicle, he doubted she had the money for such a luxury.

"I'm Marisol. Mari for short." She held out her hand to shake, and he found her grip surprisingly strong.

"Bones. And don't bother asking my birth name,

because I won't tell you."

"Fair enough." She glanced in the rear-view mirror and guided the Honda back onto the empty highway. "We don't see many natives off the reservation out here, but you're clearly not from around here. I saw your Florida license plate. Seminole?"

"Cherokee. Originally from North Carolina, but I've lived in the Keys since I left the Navy."

Mari sighed. "I've never seen the ocean. My parents were supposed to take me to Disney once when I was a kid, but my dad got drunk and wrecked our car." She shrugged as if to say, 'What are you gonna do?'

Bones managed a half-smile. "Saw plenty of that growing up. The stereotype about Indians and fire water isn't entirely undeserved."

"How about you? Do you drink?"

"I wouldn't say no to a cold one, but it's a little early in the day for a drink. How about tonight?" He glanced at the ring finger of her left hand, saw it empty, and flashed his most roguish grin in her direction.

Panic flashed across Mari's face. "Oh, I didn't mean that. I work at a bar and grill in town. The only one of either, in fact." She turned and stared into the side-view mirror. "I just thought you might like to drop in after you get your truck taken care of."

As she turned her head, Bones caught a glimpse of a bruise over her right eye. So the big sunglasses weren't solely for the purpose of keeping down the glare.

"It's cool," he said. "I've got an idea. How about, after your shift is over, I buy you a drink. Maybe whoever gave you that shiner will be stupid enough to show up and say something about it."

Mari jerked her head around, and the car swerved into the emergency lane. She overcorrected in the other direction, and Bones snatched the wheel with one hand and guided them back on course.

"I'm so sorry," she said. "I'm just really out of it today. I got this," she gestured at her eye, "rock climbing. Had a bit of a fall."

"So you don't have a boyfriend?"

"Yeah, I do."

"Is he the one who took you rock climbing?"

Mari grimaced, her jaw working for a few seconds. "The repair shop is right up there."

She nodded at a metal building with a large open bay on the front. A sun-bleached mural of hot air balloons floating across a desert landscape adorned the near side.

"Balloon Fiesta," Mari said. "They do it in Albuquerque every year. You should check it out."

"Sounds like something white people would do." Bones said, eliciting a giggle from Mari. "I might check it out if the beer is cold and the women are hot."

"So you like old, white women?" Mari teased, clearly relieved that the subject had moved away from her bruised eye.

"I just like women."

Mari pulled into the parking lot of Miguel's Automotive and Pawn. Rather, she drove off the road and onto the flat patch of dirt in front of the building, brought the car to a stop, but left the engine running. "Here's where I leave you."

"Thanks for the ride." Bones squeezed his large frame out of the Honda. He immediately felt the heat of the sun on his black hair and wondered if Manny's had air conditioning. "Where do I go if I want to get that drink later?"

"Down there on the left. It's part of the motor lodge. If you're stuck here overnight, that's the only place to stay in town."

In a different set of circumstances, Bones would have asked if she had room at her place, but the girl's situation was clearly complicated. A part of him wanted to do something about it, but he'd been in such situations before and knew how little difference his style of intervention truly made.

"All right. I might see you later."

Mari wiggled her fingers in a dainty sort of wave and drove away.

Bones managed a grin and then turned and headed for the front door of the repair shop. A sign in the dust-coated window read, "We Sell Green Chile." He pushed the door open and stuck his head inside. A glass-topped counter filled with knives, pistols, and turquoise jewelry ran across the room. Behind it, shelves piled with old DVDs, video games, and various odds and ends lined the back wall. In the corner, a gun case coated in cobwebs held a few shotguns and a single Glock.

"Lots of crap for sale, but no one to do the selling," he muttered. "Hello?" he called.

No reply.

He waited for a count of twenty before calling out again, louder this time. "Yo! Anybody here like money, because I need to spend some."

A toilet flushed somewhere behind the bookshelf. A few seconds later, a portion of shelf swung forward, and a graying man with dark brown skin and light brown teeth grinned his way into the shop.

"No need to rush me, bro. In New Mexico, we all operate on Indian time." His face went slack. "Whoa! No offense, big man."

"It's cool. My grandfather says the same thing about the reservation where I grew up. Are you Miguel?"

The man frowned and then cackled with laughter. "No way, bro. Miguel was my grandfather. I'm Manny."

"I'm Bones." They shook hands. Manny's firm, calloused grip told the tale of years of manual labor.

"You're going to stand out around here. There's only two kinds of people in Quemadura: Mexicans and Mixicans."

Bones frowned. "What's a Mixican?"

"Mexican mixed with something else." Manny cackled. "Except for the cactus, juniper, and chile, everything here is some shade of brown."

Bones decided he liked the old man in spite of his annoying laugh.

"So, what brings you in today? I don't imagine you drove here just to check out my knife collection." He tapped the glass counter with a gnarled finger, the grease under the nail forming a black crescent moon.

"Truck broke down." Bones described the problem and gave the make and model of his truck.

Manny clucked his tongue. "Should have bought a Ford."

"I'll debate you on that all day long. It's ten years old, and I've never had a problem. Until now," he added.

"Consuela's thirty years old, and she's been nothing but problems, but she still runs. Come on. We'll get your truck."

Consuela was a battered Ford pickup whose brown paint blended seamlessly into the landscape. Manny kept up a steady stream of chatter about the menu at the Blue Corn Grill where Mari worked. He recommended the cheese quesadilla, primarily because he had his doubts about the meat served up at the town's only diner.

"You ever see a roof rat? Grande! Everybody's got them. My place has got them. The motor court's got them. But Blue Corn? No roof rats. Think about that. Where do they go?"

"Into the burritos?" Bones guessed.

"Bingo."

Bones vowed to stick to beer and chips until he got back onto the road.

Half an hour later, after towing Bones' truck back to the shop and giving it a quick inspection, Manny delivered the news Bones had feared.

"You dropped your tranny, bro."

Under a different set of circumstances, he would have turned that phrase into a perverse joke, but when it meant he had to pony up the cash for a new transmission, humor was in short supply. There went most of what he'd planned on spending in Vegas.

"How soon can you have it ready?"

Manny considered the question. "I can get the parts day after tomorrow. I can have the work done the next day, assuming my nephew's sober enough to help me."

Bones resisted the urge to roll his eyes. This was, after all, the smallest of small towns. "Looks like I'll be hanging around town for a few days. Any suggestions on how to kill time?"

Manny shrugged. "I think the motor inn has HBO."

Bones gathered his belongings, thanked Manny for his help, and headed off down the road toward the motor inn. The heat rising up from the asphalt shimmered, giving the town a slightly out of focus quality. One hour ago he'd been on his way to Sin City to reconnect with an old flame. Now he was facing three days of zero kicks on Route 66. Sometimes life sucked.

Enjoyed the preview? Pick up your copy of *The Book of Bones* today!

ABOUT THE AUTHOR

David Wood is the author of the bestselling Dane Maddock Adventures and Dane Maddock Origins series and many other titles. Writing as David Debord, he writes the Absent Gods fantasy series. When not writing he hosts the Wood on Words podcast and co-hosts the Authorcast podcast. David and his family live in Santa Fe,New Mexico.

Visit him online at www.davidwoodweb.com.